D0993843

Keeping it Real

Also by Grace Dent

Keeping it Real

Grace Dent

Hodder
Children's
Books

A division of Hachette Children's Books

Copyright © 2009 Grace Dent

First published in Great Britain in 2009
by Hodder Children's Books

The right of Grace Dent to be identified as the author of
this work has been asserted by her in accordance with the
Copyright, Designs and Patents Act 1988.

1

All rights reserved. Apart from any use permitted under UK copyright
law, this publication may only be reproduced, stored or transmitted,
in any form, or by any means with prior permission in writing from the
publishers or in the case of reprographic production in accordance
with the terms of licences issued by the Copyright Licensing Agency
and may not be otherwise circulated in any form of binding or cover
other than that in which it is published and without a similar condition
being imposed on the subsequent purchaser.

All characters in this publication are fictitious and any resemblance
to real persons, living or dead, is purely coincidental.

A Catalogue record for this book is available from the British Library

ISBN-13: 978 0 340 97065 2

Typeset in New Baskerville by Avon DataSet Ltd,
Bidford-on-Avon, Warwickshire

Printed in the UK by CPI Bookmarque, Croydon, CR0 4TD

The paper and board used in this paperback by Hodder Children's Books
are natural recyclable products made from wood grown in
sustainable forests. The manufacturing processes conform to the
environmental regulations of the country of origin.

Hodder Children's Books
A division of Hachette Children's Books
338 Euston Road, London NW1 3BH
An Hachette Livre UK Company

For Clark

This diary belongs to:

Lady Shiznizz Woodizzle

Address: 34, Thundizzle Road,
            Goodmayes,
            Essex,
            BRAP 100

DECEMBER

MONDAY 24TH DECEMBER

11.55pm – St. Kevin's Church – Goodmayes – Essex. Midnight mass.

Dear Baby Jesus Lord Above.

Aight? It's Shiraz here. Shiraz Bailey Wood! How's it going, bruv? I thought I'd just take a few moments during this proper dull bit in the Christmas Eve midnight mass thingybob to wish you happy birthday and all that. Oh and to have a quick chat with you about life and, erm, for some forgiveness and stuff. 'Cos apparently that's what you hand out to folk who really want it, don't you? Forgiveness. That's about the only thing I remember from GCSE when I was at Mayflower Academy. Well that, and the fact Mrs Radowitz used to tell me to shut up and sit down all the time. Flaming liberty, eh? She wanted a bit of forgiveness herself, she did. She was always leaving crafty bottom burps in the stationary cupboard and blaming them on the drains.

OH MY DAYZ I don't know what was moving within her Lord but it certainly wasn't the holy spirit.

Anyway, look, I know it must feel like I only talk to you when I want something, and that's a bit cheeky innit?

Especially 'cos the rest of the time I go round saying I ain't totally one hundred percent you exist. But then sometimes when I'm having a right nightmare in my life I find myself saying, 'Oh Jesus Lord help me!' and proper praying that someone up above will swoop in like an X-Man and sort it out. Like that time my big sister Cava-Sue was nine months preggo and she starts making a sound like an angry cow and she slides down the side of the cooker and starts pushing her baby out on the kitchen floor!! That was well scary. I was proper praying then. But then everything turned out OK and Fin arrived and he's amazing.

And what about that morning last week when I woke up and thought I'd discovered an extra nipple growing on my chest!? Well OH MY LIFE I was freaking out big time 'cos it looked really really disgusting and let's be honest here Baby Jesus, three nipples ain't EVER a good look is it, not under any circumstances?? I ain't never seen a bikini down Top Shop with room for two normal tits and then another random one growing somewhere near my bellybutton.

So anyways, I was starting to hyperventilate and saying every prayer I could imagine and even one to Allah too 'cos I wanted to cover all bases, but then THANK GOD I remembered I'd been eating Maltesers in bed the night before and it was just a stray one that had rolled down my pyjama top, wedged under my boob and melted.

Allelujah, Lord Above! I was a two-nippled girl

6

once again. Goodmayes Girls Run Ting with totally normal baps!

The rest of the time, truth to tell, I ain't much of a God-botherer. In fact, the only reason the entire Wood family are all in church tonight sitting here like a row of lemons watching the Reverend Alan Peacock faffing about with that donkey he's borrowed from Ilford Community Petting Farm is 'cos of our Ritu.

Ritu is the little Japanese girl stood beside me now who was singing well loud to *Silent Night* just then, except not really singing anything like the tune but proper enjoying herself, she's my brother Murphy's bird from Osaka in Japan. Ritu loves Christmas to bits.

'Essex in December is BARE JOKES Shiraz!' Ritu said to me today when we were wrapping our pressies. 'It's so funny! I love all special traditions Essex people do for son of God's birthday! I love the big plastic tree in the middle of shopping mall with the lights that only work for a few days then blow fuse! And I love when your friend Carrie's dad put millions of lights on front of house and reindeer on roof and it cause traffic jam in street and neighbours all shout at him and police come! Ha ha! And every year drunk person jumps over fence and steals little plastic Baby Jesus from the crib and takes home! Very naughty!'

'Yeah, that happened again last week,' I giggled. 'It turned up in Cash Converters.'

'And I like it when the hoodies thieve box of Calgon washing machine tablets,' smiled Ritu. 'And they throw them in in the fountain by Boots and it all go all fizzy and foam go everywhere! It looks just like snow! It's so pretty! And those little green vegetable things that we eat on Christmas Day that make the big bottom gas!'

'Brussel sprouts?' I said. 'Sprouts ming BIG TIME Ritu.'

'Yes! Sprouts! They taste of boiled bogeys you always say, isn't it!?' she laughed, 'And best of all, that time when we go to church at midnight and the funny man in the black dress made the donkey come into the church and it did big poo. And then we sang the Christmas song about three kings and the Wonderbra.' Well this one had me confused, then I clicked what she meant.

'Oh yeah Ritu, *We Three Kings of Orient Are*! The Christmas carol!' I laughed. 'Actually . . . those words about the Wonderbra aren't the real words though. That's just Murphy being silly. The song is about the wise men visiting Jesus after he was born. But they didn't really "come on their scooters pipping their hooters wearing their Wonderbras".'

'Oh, they not real words?' said Ritu.

'No,' I said, while wrapping a bottle of whiskey in silver snowman paper for my father, 'the real words are quite boring. It's about them "following yonder star". I don't know what the kings wore really. I don't think they wore bras.'

'Ah . . . I like the silly words better,' Ritu said to me. 'That's what I love about being here in Essex

8

with the Wood family. It always silly. Never, ever boring.'

She looked a bit sad when she said that, 'cos of what's going on right now which made me sad too.

'Yeah, you're right,' I said to her. 'It's a lot of things living here with the Wood family but it ain't ever boring.'

So anyway, Baby Jesus, Ritu wanted us all to come to midnight mass and to be quite frank we're letting Ritu do pretty much anything she feels like right now 'cos her Tourist Visa ran out last September and immigration services are starting to get well moody about it. It's all quite heavy to be honest. Ritu don't want to go home 'cos she loves our Murph, and Murph don't want her to go 'cos he loves her. But taking all the love out of the story for a minute, the truth is we're all scared that they're going to come round and shove Ritu in one of them detention centres where she's locked up in a cell for twenty-three hours a day with only one hour free to play ping pong and do a quick poo.

I don't feel very Christmassy at all just thinking about this.

Even my mother, Diane Wood, is sad about all this Ritu stuff. Oh by the way, sorry my mother didn't make it right though the service. She left just after the first prayer 'cos she was gasping for a ciggie and the vicar took proper offence when she tried to light a Benson and Hedges off the altar candle then keep it up her sleeve.

' 'Ere Shiraz,' my mother says to me last night. 'I hope those immigration busybodies don't catch our Ritu.'

'Mother,' I laughed. 'You love it when the immigration lot catch people! When they caught that bunch of Kurdistanis living above the kebab shop you were cheering! You went down Iceland and made a little buffet!'

'Well, this is different,' tutted my mother, 'Ritu might be one of them foreigns, but she's OUR foreign and we love the bones of her.'

Now, believe me Baby Jesus, this is probably the softest thing I've ever heard my mother say. This is a woman who claims that if they brought back public hanging she'd take a day off from the betting shop and sit on the front row with some pork pies and her knitting. My mother is rock hard.

The world is proper unfair sometimes, innit? And this Ritu thing is a good example of world unfairness. 'Cos on one hand you've got all these moaning gits like my Aunty Glo saying how crap Britain is and how she's leaving and moving to Benidorm 'cos 'This country's gone to the bloody dogs' and is 'full of paedos and terrorists on benefits.' Then on the OTHER hand you've got our Ritu and she loves everything about Great Britain and she doesn't want to leave one little bit but she's getting kicked out!

I wish I made the rules sometimes.

Now and then I dream that one day I will. Believe me Britain would be a proper different land if Shiraz Bailey Wood gets to be Prime Minister. I've tried talking to my boyfriend Wesley Barrington Bains II about stuff but it doesn't go so well.

''Ere Wes,' I says to him the other day, 'the world is full of injustice, innit!? Do you think modern man can really change this through debates and laws and stuff or is it just the way life is? I can't work it out Wes, can you?'

But Wes just looks at me funny when I say stuff like that, then he told me to shush 'cos it was *Pimp My Ride* Weekend on MTV and it was the bit where Westwood and his mates have just superglued a dried ice machine on to the bonnet of an old Golf GTI and let the smoke whoosh out and all the blokes were proper sobbing and bro-hugging each other with solid gold happiness. Wes loves that bit in *Pimp My Ride*. I would have felt bad if I'd shouted at him to press pause on the Sky Plus and bloody listen to me for a minute.

Bless Wes though, eh Lord? I do love him though. Honest I do. I think. He keeps saying we should get a Staffordshire bull terrier puppy at the moment and keep it at his house and it could be our dog and we could look after it together. I ain't sure if that's a good idea to be honest, for more reasons than one. Anyways ... I'm getting off the point. I know you're a well busy person Lord above, so I won't take up any more of your time when you should be healing the sick or keeping an eye on all the headcases down Ilford Wetherspoons who've been getting plastered on the Two for One 'Holy Spirit' offers and are now having trouble getting home without getting happy-stabbed or run over by a truck or just widdling in their own trousers on the nightbus. I don't envy your job sometimes, it's well responsible. Here's those things I wouldn't mind a bit of holy forgiveness for:

First of all, I wouldn't mind a bit of forgiveness for some of the proper unkind thoughts I've been having about my mother of late. OH MY LIFE she is doing my head in! And yes, yes I know you're meant to 'Honour Thy Father and Mother' but ever since I moved back into Thundersley Road last January, she's stepped up her annoyingness to an all new head-bending level. In fact, sometimes I have to get up off the sofa and walk out of the front door and stand in the front garden by the wheelie bin counting slowly to ten to calm down!

My good mate Uma Brunton-Fletcher taught me to do this as an 'anger management technique' and it must work 'cos Uma ain't a mentaloid any more and she's got a brilliant job in a casino and a flat in London and she's driving a proper blinged up 4x4 with blackened windows and she ain't been lifted on a Saturday night for chucking Smirnoff Ice bottles at fire engines for AGES. That was old Uma. New Uma is a different person ever since she got control of her anger and channelled it into something positive.

So I'm doing a lot of counting to ten right now. Like the other night when my mother started wigging on at me for the twentieth time that I want to get myself engaged to to Wesley Barrington Bains, 'cos Wesley's the best boy I'll ever manage to get what with me 'coming from a very plain family of women who always end up with big fat bums and arms like pork sausages and facial hair problems by the time they're thirty-five!'

Oh my life! She actually said this. Honest to God, she's insane. INSANE IN THE BRAIN.

'You wanna get a ring on that finger sooner rather than later Shiraz! That's another year you've let slip by! Wasn't it last Christmas that you and Cava-Sue reckoned he was about to propose!?' she was quacking on. 'What you being so fussy for!? Wesley's a proper good catch he is! He's got a skill! He's a plumber! What he don't know about mending a toilet ain't worth knowing! 'Ere, I can't even count the amount of times this family would have been sitting with our legs crossed and our back teeth floating if he'd not come in and mended our lavvy! What a star!'

'Gngngngngn, can you get out of the way of the telly mother,' I mumbled, trying to watch *Hollyoaks*.

'And Wesley's got his own flat too!' she says. 'He's on the property ladder! You wouldn't have to be working down at Lidl for much longer if you got yourself married! Oh Shiraz, I'd have given my right arm for a bloke like Wesley when I was young. When me and your dad got wed we had to live with your nan for two years and I could hear her grinding her teeth every night through the bedroom wall! Couldn't I Brian?'

My father didn't say anything to all of this. He quite

likes it when it's me getting nagged 'cos it gives him a bit of downtime to read the *Ilford Bugle* in peace.

'Oh shut up, Mother! SHUT UP!' I shouted eventually. 'I'm happy as I am! I like working at Lidl! I've only just turned twenty years old. I'm still a child! I've got my whole life to live. I am on a voyage of self-discovery! Leave me alone!'

'Pah! Self-discovery!' my mother says nearly choking, 'Well all I'm saying is that just you watch how quickly you "discover" how twenty years old becomes thirty, then thirty becomes forty-five and then where will you be!? Eh? Like your Aunty Patricia! Living in a house that smells of cat widdle with three cats and her boobs all gone droopy down by her knees and no bloke to share her life with! You think on about that, Shiraz Bailey Wood! Do you know what your Aunty Pat is doing special for Christmas this year?! Do you, eh? She's fitting her spare room with special heated bunk beds and a play area for her cats! Bunk beds?! FOR CATS!!! She bought them on-line from a luxury pet shop in Sweden! That place must make a killing at Christmas from lonely spinsters who thought they were too good to settle down with decent boys when they were young! 'Ere, that's an idea, I'll get Aunty Glo to write you down the details!!! w bloody w bloody bleeding dot bleeding I'm going end up sad and on my jack jones dot bleeding com!'

Well at this point, dear Lord, I went to stand by the wheelie bin for a bit and cool down, but as I was going

14

she shouted at me, 'You remember what I said, Shiraz! You'll think back on this when I'm dead and gone!'

My mother is not dying, by the way. She's only forty-eight. There's at least fifty years left in her yet. She just likes to remind us all now and then that she'll be dead soon, 'cos she knows it shakes us up. Dear Baby Jesus if you're listening to this, please give me loads of patience to get through Christmas without any big arguments. Please let us all have a Happy Christmas, please, thank you, ta.

Oh and another thing, I'm aware that I've not been being totally truthful with my best mate Carrie Draper of late. In fact, I've been lying. I think there's a name for this sort of lie I've been telling her, ain't there. It's called a white lie, innit? That's when you really want to keep it real but you know the realness will get you into all sorts of trouble.

So when Cazza says to me, ''Ere, Shizzle, do you think my bum's got bigger since I got back with my Bezzie Kelleher and he's started delivering for Dominos and keeps bringing me extra pizzas and tubs of my favourite Ben and Jerry's Chunky Monkey ice cream every night? What do you think, look!?'

Then she bends over in her trousers and puts her behind in my face!

Well I haven't got the heart to say, 'Yeah, definitely, it's about twice as big.' So I say, 'No Cazza, you still look exactly the same!'

And I definitely don't let her know that when our Murphy saw a recent picture I had of Carrie on my camera he said, 'Holy crap, Shiz, is that Carrie!? Is she wearing one of them sumo suits?! Man she's is well bigger than she used to be!'

So I told our Murph to shut up and said it ain't nice to call anyone sumo and at least she weren't being all anorexic and ill now, and obsessed with her body like she was last year when she was living on half a grapefruit and three diet pills a day and running six miles before she has the grapefruit. 'Cos now Carrie is back with Bezzie and happy and in love. She is well loved up at the moment so I'm just happy that she's happy. And Bezzie has got a job and started showering more regular again and stopped turning up at my Wesley's flat in just a hoodie and his pyjamas bottoms 'cos he can't be arsed to get dressed. And he hasn't got yellow teeth covered in bits of Pot Noodle any more, so I feel like they're both making some progress in their lives and that is a GOOD THING.

'Fair play, sis,' Murphy says to me. 'But one thing, eh? If she comes over this Christmas don't be giving her the Quality Street tin before I've had all my share of the green triangles! In fact, save up all those well hard toffee pennies that no one likes that are always still here in January 'cos Cazza looks like she could manage a dozen of them in one go!'

And OK, that was quite funny but I didn't giggle 'cos Cazza is still my best mate and you don't giggle at your best mate's bum getting bigger even if she did put on a pair of white trousers the other day and when she bent over her butt reminded me of the mega-screen down at Vue cinema. Oh God I'm going to hell for thinking that, ain't I? But believe me I'm sorry about the lying. I'm telling a lot of lies right now. A LOT. I lie all the time. I ain't keeping it real at all, like, EVER.

Like when I say to Murphy that I'm sure this thing with Ritu is going to be fine and I'm totally confident that the Brunton-Fletcher family down the road can MAKE Ritu a fake passport, well OH MY DAYS, I don't mean that at all, 'cos I've seen little Reuben Brunton-Fletcher's first attempt and basically it was just the cardboard from an old Coco Pops box coloured in with magic markers with a photo of Jet Li stuck to it. Jet Li don't look like our Ritu at all! Jet Li is a bloke! This was NOT the work of master forgery, I'll tell you that for nothing, blud.

And when Cava-Sue says to me, 'Ere Shiraz, was Fin good for you today?! Did you give him those Organic sugar free biscuits and do those baby yoga positions that I told you!' Well I say, 'Yes, Cava-Sue, that's what we did! He loved it!' and I don't tell her that I stuck on *Balamory* the moment she left and we both shared some ASDA chocolate trifle and then he ran around with a pan on his head butting things for five hours. I don't tell her any of that. I am such a LIAR LIAR THONG ON FIRE!

And when I was doing my Christmas shopping last week I kept saying to all the family that I'd not be buying anyone very much 'cos money is a bit tight this year what with Lidl not paying very much money for shelf-stacking, well this was a BIG FAT LIE too 'cos I do have some money! In fact I've got a secret on-line bank account that nobody knows about. I've got over seven and a half grand! It makes my heart go all bumpy and fluttery to think about it. But no one knows about it except Tiffany Poole who I was working for earlier this year when I earned it and it's not like she'll even remember 'cos she's got billions and billions of pounds herself and is too busy having her nose cosmetically relocated about her face and her boobs raised and lowered.

But the thing is I need the money, Lord above! I do! I need to save it 'cos I've got a big secret plan. And I know my family would really love to get their hands on it 'cos they've never ever had any proper money in their lives either, but the fact is that if this plan comes together then one day I'll make enough money to treat them to whatever they bloody want.

Trust me on that one, I will.

It's another of those white lie things, innit? And I'm sorry about all the lying, honest I am, 'cos it don't make me feel good at all. In fact it makes me feel very bad. And I'm extra specially very, very sorry that since September I've been putting on that Lidl uniform and going downstairs of a morning and eating toast with my mum and Cava-Sue and then saying 'See ya everyone! I'm off to work now!' and then popping back up to my room and grabbing my big bag which is always well heavy with all the things I need for that day and then I walk out of the door and most of the time I don't go to Lidl 'cos I work about eight hours there a week . . . the rest of the time I'm at my secret place doing secret stuff.

You know where I mean.

Special secret stuff! It's the biggest secret ever. So Baby Jesus up above, if you are listening to this, I'm sorry about all the lying, but basically I've figured out that sometimes if you want to keep it real and stay true to your dreams you've got to tell some really big whopping lies and . . . and . . . OH MY DAYS . . . Hang on a minute? Where have all my family gone? Hang on, the church is empty! How long have I been sitting here? Oooh flipping heck I better go and catch everyone up. Thank you for listening Lord! Here's wishing you a merry shizmas and a happy new year and all that, AMEN!

TUESDAY 25TH DECEMBER – CHRISTMAS DAY

11pm – in my bedroom.

Ahhh, today was proper brilliant. One of the nicest Christmas Days ever. There was a well happy chilled out atmosphere most of the day and no silly rows. GO TEAM WOOD! WELL DONE ALL OF US! One of the most most amazing things about Christmas these days is that we've got our Fin now who's only two years old and when you see how excited he gets about things, even though he's too young to understand most of it, well it makes everyone else start buzzing their heads off with the Christmas vibe too. When I see Fin's little face, it reminds me of how I used to feel back in the day when Christmas felt all magical and you couldn't sleep for counting off the other sleeps you had to get through to it!

Back then, me, Cava-Sue and Murph all knew Santa was coming but we just couldn't work out how! How could this bloke on a sledge who'd never met us know our names and work out if we'd been bad or good!? And how was he going to get a whole sack of pressies down the chimney when we had a gas fire that was glued to the wall? And how was he going to visit every kid in the world and still have time to feed his reindeer with the carrots that we left out for him on the mantelpiece?

Stuff like this used to drive us all mad trying to work it out. But then we got older and Christmas started to lose its sparkle, especially since me and Murph and Cava-Sue all stopped believing in Santa, which meant that when mother stuck out a mince pie and a carrot on a plate and some sherry on the mantelpiece for Santa and said, 'Ooh fancy that, I wonder who ate that?!' Well we'd all look at her and go, 'Erm, you and Aunty Glo? We heard you laughing when you were doing it. Glo left a lipstick smear on the plate.'

And when it came time for the pressies to be opened, there wouldn't that Santa bag full of toys and games waiting for me like when I was tiny, it would be sensible stuff like I got today which included a new wastepaper bin for my bedroom (No really. A bin. Even if it was pink with hearts on it, it was still a bloody BIN). And some big beige support knickers that start at my bellybutton and stretch halfway down my thighs from Murphy, 'So you can eat as many pies as you want and not have a fat bum, innit.'

Ritu apologised afterwards, she'd told him to get me a scarf.

Or a one-thousand-piece jigsaw of a squirrel from my Nan with a fiver taped to the front. Bless her, I reckon she was having one of her senior moments when she bought me that.

Christmas certainly gets less Christmassy I reckon when you get older, don't it? In fact, by the time I was about fifteen Christmas just started being a whole lot of arguments with my mum about whether I was allowed to go to Christmas parties or not. (No, we were too young.) And whether I could drink booze when I got there (No we were DEFINITELY too young). Then, what time we had to come back again if we got there. (Ten o clock! OH MY DAYS. What's the bloody point of going!??)

One of the worst Christmas Days we had was about six years ago my mother and Cava-Sue spent all day in the proper hump with each other 'cos my mother had caught Cava-Sue at 3am that morning snogging a bloke called TJ who she'd met at Faces in Gants Hill on the bonnet of next door's Volvo Estate! She'd been at a party with her mate Collette Brown and copped off with him and they'd shared a taxi home!

Well when my mother saw Cava-Sue 'canoodling' she shouted out of the window really loud, 'CAVA-SUE GET YOUR SELF INDOORS NOW YOU ARE A DISGRACE!' and then TJ ran off and Cava-Sue fell off the bonnet with a massive thud and set off next door's car alarm and then she just lay in the snow for a while waving her legs about in the air shouting, 'Happy Chrishmtmashhh Thundersley Road! Look at me! I am totally lying on the road! I am so DRUNKSH! How do you like that Bert at eighty-nine you nosy old fart!?? Here's something for you to tell the council about!!'

Well this was bad enough, but then the next day when Cava-Sue came down for Christmas dinner she was wearing this weird flouncy neck scarf and my mum starts saying, 'Why are you dressed like a fool Cava-Sue, what's under that neck scarf?!' Well it turned out to be a MASSIVE LOVEBITE. Ha ha ha ha ha! OH MY DAYS my mother was furious. Well it all kicked off then and lots of stuff was said that wasn't Christmassy in the slightest and mother and Cava-Sue never exchanged their pressies until January 2nd!

But those days are over now 'cos we've got Fin and he's put the Christmas magic back in Christmas. 'Cos each night when we put the tree lights on at night he stands in front of it in his little all-in-one tiger-striped bedtime suit and his little face is proper cute when he watches the lights twinkling and says, 'Treesh, treesh!' like he's trying to get his head round why there's a tree there.

And when he sees the bags of food coming in from Iceland and the extra-special ones that my mother brings in from Marks and Spencer that have some posh puddings in that we only ever get once a year as a special treat 'cos they are mega-expensive, well Fin starts grabbing at the bag and shouting, 'Pubbing! Pubbbbing!?'

And after seeing the puddings he refuses to eat any of his organic vegetable casserole what Cava-Sue has cooked him what looks and smells just exactly like curried earwax. He's got his eye on something much more exciting instead!

And last night when Fin saw the little dish on the mantelpiece with the carrot for Rudolph and Santa's mince pie he got proper giddy. Then he ran to the window and he looked at the black sky and the stars and shouted 'Shanta! Shaaanta! Shaaaaaaanta!??' about a million times till his little cheeks were all red and his eyes were proper big like he was off his head on pure joy. It's proper IMPOSSIBLE to not think Christmas feels a bit more magical when there's a little person running about.

We were all up really extra early this morning 'cos Fin wanted to get out of his cot at six o clock and he was shouting as loud as he could the whole range of the seventeen words that he sort of knows.

Cava-Sue gave up trying to shush him in the end and

carried him downstairs and Lewis followed her and soon there was a massive buzz going on with Cava-Sue and Lewis shouting, 'Oh my dayz! Fin! He's been! He's been! Santa came to Essex!'

And then my mother appears 'cos she didn't want to miss Fin opening his presents and she starts shouting on Dad to get up and check on the turkey which was defrosting in the bath and then Murph and Ritu appeared to see what all the noise was and before I knew it the whole Wood family were all in the living room and the TV was blaring proper loud with *A Muppet Christmas Carol* on Sky One and someone had the Quality Street tin out and our silly fat Staffy Penny was running around begging chocolates.

So I put the kettle on and made us a pot of tea and Murphy opened his new Playstation game he'd got from Mum and Dad called Pirate Bloodbath II and him and Lewis both plonked down on the sofa trying to work out how to play it. My mother seemed a bit quiet now compared to usual so I says, ''Ere are you feeling OK?'

'Yeah,' she said. 'I've just got a bit of pain in my side. I reckon it's those prawns I ate last night that I got reduced down Kwiksave.' Then she smiled to show me that she was OK again.

So then Dad appears from upstairs where he was on turkey duties, trying to wind everyone up that the turkey has done a runner and we're all going to have to ring Dominos for a pizza instead and then he puts on that *A*

Right Rollicking Christmas Party CD that we play every year with the song by that ancient band Wham my mother likes called *Last Christmas*, and he pulled Mum up off the couch and made her dance with him in their dressing gowns and my mother said he was a silly old git but she danced with him anyway.

Then Cava-Sue let Fin open his first gift from Santa which was a big yellow truck what he could sit on with a proper noisy horn. Well Fin LOVED the truck and he climbed on to the back of it and spent the next two hours pushing himself around on the truck smashing into the video cabinet and crashing into the sofa, honking the horn again and again and getting told to be careful by everyone and ignoring us all totally until eventually Cava-Sue started saying we should call Toys R Us and see if they were open 'cos she wanted to get him a crash helmet.

Then my dad pipes up, 'Oh he's only a little lad ain't he? He's bound to have a broken arm or something at one point. It's all part of life!'

Then Cava-Sue went white as a sheet and said, 'Fin ain't that type of little boy, Father! Fin is a very sensitive child! I reckon he might be a poet or a ballet dancer when he grows up actually!' Well we all had to stop ourselves laughing when she said that 'cos Fin ain't delicate at all he's like World Wrestling Entertainment in a babygro!

Then it was my mother's turn to open her pressies from us. She'd got a big bottle of her favourite peppermint foot scrub from Murph and Ritu and a new, furry hot water bottle from Cava-Sue, Lewis and Fin. I'd got her some of those books she loves reading from Asda which are in the 'Tragic Life Stories' section which are all about people who have had proper tragic childhoods and have been locked in cupboards and fed dog biscuits and hidden in attics for years on end and they want to tell you about it for three hundred and fifty pages and make you as depressed as they are. My mother loves these books. She reads shedloads of them. They're always called proper sad names like *The Stranger Next Door* or *The Child Who No one Loves* or *Ooh Mummy, Please Don't Stuff Me Back In The Cellar*! And the covers are well depressing and OH MY DAYZ my mother loves them. She enjoys nothing more than an early night reading one of these books getting proper wound up about them! Then she swaps the ones she's finished with my Aunty Glo and they both phone each other up of a night trading stories of terrible doom. Bless my mother, she loves a bit of misery, she does.

So this morning my mother unwrapped her books and looked at the covers and she seemed proper touched, then she smiled and said, ''Ere, Shiraz darling. Thank you. These were the ones I said I wanted ages ago! That's proper thoughtful, that is!' Then she did something really strange. She got up, walked across the room and kissed me on the forehead.

Now my mother hardly ever really kisses me. Not that

she don't love me 'cos she does, I know she does, but she's not a kissy-wissy person. Then she looked at all her pressies and she looked at Fin playing on his truck and says, 'You're a wonderful family, you lot are. You do me proud.' Well we all stopped what we were doing and looked at her a bit funny. Again, this was a bit weird, but at the same time it felt nice. Proper Christmassy. Then she said ''Ere Brian, go and fetch the camera. I want a picture of all of us together on Christmas Day.'

So we all jammed on to the sofa and put our arms round each other and my dad snapped some pictures.

Then Lewis got hold of the camera and took some more, with my father in too. And in some of the pictures our Murphy was making rude signs behind Lewis's head. And in other ones Cava-Sue had her eyes shut, and in one of them I had a double chin and it looked like my finger was half up my nose, but on the last one we all looked really happy and together like a proper family.

My mother looked at that one for a long time and then her eyes seemed to go all watery and she said, 'That's lovely that one is, I'm going to get a frame for that,' and then she went a bit quiet.

Now I come to think about it, that picture part was a bit strange. Happy but a little bit sad too. I can't put my finger on why.

Oh, I'm just being silly, I reckon. I think too much, that's what Wesley always tells me. It annoys me a little bit when he says that to be frank, 'cos how do you stop your head thinking? Surely thinking is a good thing. You can't do too much thinking I reckon.

So anyway, the rest of the day has been nice. Chilled out, even. 'Cos oddly enough it turned out that the turkey hadn't done a runner down Goodmayes High Street, so we ate it with some chipolata sausages and stuffing and parsnips and roast spuds. And Nan and Clement came for dinner and at first Nan was in a bit of a huff with Clement, 'cos apparently their Tuesday club had gone on their Christmas outing to Harry Ramsdens Fish and Chip Restaurant at Thurrock for a 'sing-a-long special' the night before, and Clement had drunk too much Guinness and sung-along far louder than he should have and 'caused a spectacle of himself', but then she forgot about it and forgave him.

And as usual Murphy called the parsnips 'PARP-snips' and made farty sounds whenever anyone reached for one. And as usual no one really fancied the christmas pudding and brandy custard but then they ate some anyway.

Then at about 6pm my Wesley Barrington Bains II came over looking all smart and smelling of his new Hugo Boss aftershave that I got him on special offer down TK Maxx. Everyone was really happy to see Wes, 'cos they always are. It's like he's a bloody celebrity or something.

But by this time the whole Wood family was totally

cream-crackered knackered and we were all sitting in a big heap in front of *EastEnders* eating Ferrero Rocher. We burned ourselves out much too early. We were all ready for bed!

Wesley gave me some nice pressies. A pair of gorgeous dangly diamond earrings from H. Samuel what I'd pointed out and said I liked once when there was a leaflet with them on in the *News Of The World*. And some Nike trainers that I've had my eye on for about six weeks but I thought were just too crazy expensive. One hundred and fifty quid! Wes spoils me so much. I do love him to bits sometimes.

'Oh my life! Thank you Wes!' I said to him and gave him a cuddle. I felt a proper pang of guilt then. I've been telling him so many lies too. That ain't good is it? I'm doing it for the best, though. Honest I am.

'Happy Christmas Shizzle,' he said to me. 'I knew you wanted those trainers, innit.' Then he pulled me in closer so only I could hear and says, 'I got another gift for you but I'll give you it another time, innit.'

'What gift?' I whispered. 'What do you mean?'

'It's a secret, innit,' he said. 'Now ain't the right time.'

I looked at him funny when he said that. I don't know what the hell he's going on about. But I know one thing, if he's got me a Staffordshire bull terrier puppy, I'm gonna be a bit upset 'cos I LOVE staffies to bits but I don't think I've got time to devote to one properly right now. Staffies act like little kids, honest they do. They need loads of love and attention all the time. When we got our Penny, me and Cava-Sue used to stay up with her till really late at night 'cos she was scared in her basket away from her mum. Then in the end she started sleeping mostly in our beds. Our Penny won't like that new dog at all! A dog ain't just for Christmas, Wesley, it's for life. I hope my Wesley remembers that. Oh I'm too knackered to think about this now, I'm off to sleep.

THURSDAY 27TH DECEMBER

I got up early this morning and slid out of the house before anyone could start asking me too many questions about what I was up to. One of the sort of infuriating but also funny things about living with my family is that you never get to do anything EVER, without a big family debate on it. Not a sensible debate either, just everyone sticking their oar in.

I didn't realise that properly until a few years ago when me and Uma lived together in Whitechapel in London and we were lazing about on the couch one Sunday flicking through the channel and we found this opera on the telly. On BBC2 I think. I hadn't ever seen an opera before but I always wondered what went on so we tried to watch it.

Well anyway, I was laughing my head off 'cos it went on for about three hours and basically what would happen is one geezer in a big hat and silly trousers would walk on stage and he's sing in a loud booming voice:

'I am riding to the next village to find my true love! La-da-dah! Oh yes I am! Watch me go! I'm going now! Fetch me my horse. I'm off now, bye bye!'

It was all in Italian so we only knew this from the subtitles. But then about thirty other people would run in from the sides of the stage and they'd all start singing: *'Oh, he's going to the next village! Tra-la-la! Why's he going there!? Maybe we'll never know! Maybe we should ask him? Fiddle-dee-dee! He's going on his horse! Oh, the village is a long way away! I hope he's got a good horse and plenty of hay for the horse! La la la la la! Oh he's off to the next village to find his true love!!'*

What a palaver, eh? It took him about an hour to get on his horse and by that point he'd decided not to go. Me and Uma were wetting ourselves.

'That's like my house in Goodmayes,' I says to Uma. 'Cos it's like that all the time. It's one of the reasons I know that one day I should move out for good. Like today, if I'd said, 'Hey everyone I'm just popping down Ilford Mall!' then my mother would have rushed in from the kitchen and said, 'What? You're going out?! Are you sure the shops are open? And you ain't got any money! And it's raining and it's cold! You ain't got enough layers on! That hoodie ain't even waterproof! What you need is a jumper and a waterproof kagoule! 'Ere, Cava-Sue, come here a minute! Pop upstairs and lend Shiraz that waterproof kagoule!'

31

And then Cava-Sue would appear and say, 'It's not even raining Mother! It's the FROST Shiraz needs to be worried about! Shiraz didn't tell you that thirty per cent of heat is lost through the head in winter!? What you need is a hat! Why ain't you got a hat on Shiraz? Do you want to borrow my patchwork beanie hat that my mate Pixie crocheted me for Christmas from llama wool? It's lovely it is! You can still smell the llamas!'

Then my mother would start flapping saying, 'She'll be too hot in a hat, Cava-Sue! It's proper humid inside Ilford Mall! What Shiraz needs to put on is a T-shirt, then a jumper, then a jacket and take an umbrella!'

Then Cava-Sue would chip in, 'Shiraz shouldn't be going shopping anyway! Shopping in the sales is bad for the environment! None of us need anything. Why don't you stay in with me and Lewis and Fin and we can do your squirrel jigsaw!'

That's the thing about my family. They love a fuss. That's why I sort of don't tell them them things now and then. And why I sneak off before they can find out what I'm doing.

'Just going down TK Maxx to buy a dress or something for Carrie's party,' I shouted quickly to our Murph this morning then shot out the door at 9am. Carrie's parents have gone to Sandals in the Seychelles for New Year and she's having a party while they're away so it was pretty feasible that I'd be off out to the Sales. Luckily Murphy was sitting mesmerised by his Pirate game and didn't hear me go. He's built himself an entire new ship called *The Pride of Goodmayes* on *Pirate Bloodbath II* and he's been sharing it on-line, so he'd been up since 6am playing against some kid from New York. Murph's T-shirt was covered in Pop Tart crumbs and ketchup stains. I wandered down Thundersley Road. It felt good to be out in the fresh air. I stuck my iPod on and listened to some Mariah Carey as I walked down the road. I love Mariah Carey. I love that track called *I Stay In Love* where she does the well high note at the end and in the video she's a Las Vegas showgirl. She is well nang. A lot of people diss Mariah but I reckon it's mostly boys who don't like a strong woman. Mariah is proper fierce. So I wandered down towards Goodmayes Park, 'cos I thought I'd walk most of the way to Ilford 'cos I was enjoying my tunes. I walked past the duckpond and through the little kiddies' play area and then past the bandstand where me and Uma and Kez used to sit some nights when we were in Year Nine getting up to no good, back in the day before Uma became a reformed hooligan and Kez had her little girl Tiq and her new baby boy Saxon.

The bandstand looked pretty scuzzy really. The ground was covered in old chewing gum and fag packets and little puddles of frozen spit and someone had spray-painted 'ROOOOOOB-BF- KICK 2 KILL' in red paint along the side of it. It ain't that hard to figure out who 'Roob B-F' is. Everyone knows Reuben Brunton-Fletcher. He's almost as famous for being a wannabe rudeboy dipstick as his brother Clinton now. Clinton's reputation is fading a bit these days since he's been banged up for a while and rumour has it that he's been learning to read. Kezia seems to think that Clinton might get let out of jail soon for good behaviour, 'cos he's been a good boy ever since Saxon arrived. Kez says she can't wait for him to come home so her and Clinton and Tiq and Saxon can be a little family together.

This is proper committed of Kez considering how much of her social security benefits she'll lose if she has a full-time partner moving in. Maybe this time for Kezia it's true love.

I stood and stared at the bandstand for a bit, trying to remember what made me sit there all those nights freezing my arse off. Especially as the park keeper with the nose like a squashed strawberry used to show up every half hour and moan and moan, then threaten us with everything from prison to a good thrashing with a stick just for sitting there sharing one bottle of Banana Mad Dog and a ten-pack of Marlboro Lights between about twenty of us! I felt bad for him really, it was like he was going to have a heart attack. But the thing is, it wasn't really like we had anywhere else to go. 'Cos all of our mothers were sick to death of us, so if we stayed indoors they were nagging us all the time about school and stuff. And we weren't allowed our mates around the house 'cos then our parents would nag us about who we were kicking about with. None of us girls were allowed to speak to Uma Brunton-Fletcher 'cos Uma was a headcase, but then we were all too scared to tell Uma that or blank her 'cos then she'd kick off big time. And the Springfield Youth Club closed down 'cos none of the youth leaders wanted to run it any more 'cos they were sick of getting called paedos by the parents for wanting to work with kids – which they totally weren't by the way, they were just some well nice Muslim geezers who gave their time free to help the community. Then some kids vandalised the bloody hall anyhow, just for a laugh, and the council wouldn't repair it 'cos by this point Mayflower had come bottom of all the OFCOM tables and the newspapers were calling us Superchav Academy and the council wouldn't give any more money to 'youth projects' 'cos they said the kids were so 'feral' it was like 'pouring tax payers money into a big black hole'. Charming!

So that's how we all ended up sitting at the bandstand.

And we weren't really causing trouble, not most of us anyhow. I was proper quiet most of the time compared to Uma and Latoya who I admit could get a bit lairy when they'd been drinking but then if you've met Uma's and Latoya's mothers you'd know why. It ain't like they've had much example in their lives of folk NOT being lairy. OH MY DAYZ Rose Brunton-Fletcher is a beast of a woman, she really is.

So anyway, a few bad things happened down the bandstand, like the fire brigade getting called when Cassia and Ashleen made that fire out of bog-roll and

Elnett hairspray and it got out of control. And then Knighty got an ASBO and the *Ilford Bugle* started putting pictures of us with our hoods up on the front cover every night and calling us 'chavs' who 'must be stamped out'. I never thought I was a chav to be honest. I know folk used to call me one. In fact they probably still do, 'cos I don't look much different now do I? But I ain't bothered at all. They can call me what they want. It's water off a duck's back. I know who I am and that's the main thing, innit?

So I was thinking about all this when I was walking past the bandstand and thinking that if I was in power, like a politician or something who went to the Houses of Parliament and debated laws and stuff I would tell them that it's wrong to slag off kids and give them names like 'chav' or 'feral', 'cos most of them are just a bit lost and need something positive to do with their time. Well, as I was thinking that the park keeper with the nose like a strawberry came wandering out of his little hut and spotted me and shouted, 'OI! NO HOODIES ALLOWED IN THE PARK!' And I looked at him and then I remembered I was wearing my pink hoodie and you're meant to put the hood inside when you walk through the park. This is the law. HA HA HA, there is actually a sign that says it and everything. HA HA HA HA! Oh my days, grown-ups are mental! So I says, 'Oh don't worry, I'm going now anyway!' and walked off with my shoulders back and my head held high and my hoodie flapping wild and free in the breeze. I may be a hoodie but I'm not ashamed about who I am or what I look like. I'm fierce I am. Just like Mariah.

I didn't go to TK Maxx by the way. I went to the Waterstones book shop in the high street. When I got there, I put my hood up and wrapped my scarf round my face and sneaked inside 'cos I was a bit paranoid that Aunty Glo might be in town and spot me and ring a full and detailed report back to my mum.

I went to the Classic Literature section and picked out two novels by Thomas Hardy and a book about Elizabethan Britain and went to the counter and got my secret debit card out of the back section of my Burberry purse. They cost twenty three-pounds, seventy-six pence! OH MY DAYZ. Books cost a bloody fortune.

Then I left Waterstones and popped over to Wetherspoons and nipped into the ladies' loos and swapped the books into a River Island bag that I'd bought in my pocket and stuck the old Waterstones bag into the tampax bin, just like Uma used to do back in the day when she was shoplifting. Then I got the bus home carrying the River Island bag looking exactly like a girl who'd just bought a dress for a New Year's Eve party at her best mate's house. It's a bit like being James Bond sometimes, this secret mission lark.

When I got back to Thundersley Road I ran upstairs quickly and hid the books then joined my whole family who were in the living room, which was about a hundred degrees 'cos the radiators and the fire was on, all eating leftover stuffing sandwiches and pork pies and drinking mugs of tea and trying to play *Pirate Bloodbath II.*

''Ere Shiraz, where have you been!?' my mother said. 'You ain't been out dressed like that have you! Just in a hoodie? You ain't got enough layers on! You must have been freezing cold!'

'I know!' said Cava-Sue, 'Why didn't you come and borrow a hat!?'

'And a scarf! Your neck is bare!' said my mother. 'You at least needed a scarf! Your chest must have been FROZEN SOLID. 'Ere Shiraz, you want to be careful. I once saw someone on Sky News who went out without a scarf at Christmas and a cold snap started from the east all of a sudden and THEY DIED.'

'It weren't that cold,' I said, trying not to giggle. Then I got myself a cuppa and wedged in on the sofa beside my mother and tucked my cold feet under her warm bum. They drive me mental, but I do love them.

JANUARY

TUESDAY 1ST JANUARY

7am – my bedroom.

I've just woken up. Ughghg me throat hurts. I only got to sleep about three hours ago and I forgot to take my mascara and eye-liner off so it's all over the place. I look well gothic actually, proper dramatic. I was at Carrie Draper's New Year's Eve extravaganza last night and it all got a bit messy. Oh my dayz. What have I done? Oh God. I reckon there's a strong chance I might have done something proper daft. It's starting to come back to me now. It's not like it was ME who did the daft thing . . . I just didn't stop the daft thing from going any further. I was a bit tipsy. This is why I hardly EVER drink booze. Booze makes you do stupid things and act like a knobber and honest to God I am enough of a knobber already. When people take the mick out of me for hardly ever drinking I tell them this to shut them up. Oh flipping heck. I hope Wesley don't remember anything of what got said at the end of last night.

He won't will he?

Nah, he won't.

He can't. He was totally steamboats, off on another planet. Him and Bezzie had been drinking cans of Stella and doing Tequila shots every half hour from 9pm to midnight. Wes was slurring his words and calling me 'Shillaz' and challenging Bezzie to a breakdancing 'Dance Off' to old-skool hip hop from the nineties.

My Wes CAN'T breakdance by the way. Not one bit. He just jerks his arms and legs about like he's being electrocuted and pretends to be a robot by moving his head from side to side and saying 'I AM A ROBOT' in the voice of a robot. It's funny 'cos he's totally rubbish and he knows he is, but he pulls this face like he thinks he's good. Everyone at Carrie's party was properly in hysterics cheering him on, which he loved, of course. My Wesley is like a different person when he's got booze inside him. That's why Bezzie always encourages Wes to drink too much, 'cos it brings out this other version of Wes that's hiding inside him. To be honest though, I like normal Wesley that I see every day much better. 'Cos normal Wesley is proper chilled out and sensible and would never have started telling me all those things tonight and making me make promises that I don't know if I can keep.

Oh, this is my making excuses, innit. I can't blame him, I should have set him straight but I didn't. I AM SUCH A KNOBBER.

I'll go back to the the beginning. Tonight started off really lovely 'cos I started getting glammed up really early by having a long bath with loads of my new special Clinique bath soak that Carrie got me for Christmas.

Amazing. I managed to stay in there for FORTY-FOUR WHOLE MINUTES without anyone banging on the door demanding that I get out 'cos they need to have a wee, squeeze a spot or read the back of the Radox bottle.

Or as Murph just does, walk straight in and start doing a massive wee in the loo beside me 'cos Murphy has no concept of personal space whatsoever. In fact if he did have any concept of keeping his private life private then I wouldn't have to sleep with a Lillet tampon in each ear and a balaclava on, 'cos I can hear him and Ritu squelching away next door when I'm trying to get to sleep three inches away through the wall. (Vomit x100000000000.)

So anyway, I had a long uninterrupted bath tonight and it was well nice. One day I'd love to have my own home with a nice bathroom with one of them big white porcelain baths like Tiffany Poole has that stands alone on little gold feet and a lock on the door that works. I wouldn't want Tiffany Poole's life at all but I'd like little bits of it.

I lay in the bath until my skin went all wrinkly like an old peach and then I got out and wrapped myself in a warm towel I'd hung up on the radiator and covered myself in that lovely smelling Tiffany Poole body moisturiser which is called 'Gush: Creme De Enlightenment.' Apparently if you rub enough on your body it's got 'special vitamins that seep through the epidermis of your skin and then stimulate your brain cells to give you a deeper understanding of your life.' Ha ha ha. No seriously, this is what it says on the bottle.

I tried telling Tiffany that the 'enlightenment' part ain't possible 'cos science-wise I don't think you can absorb vitamins through your skin that do anything to your brain cells but she weren't listening to me properly. I think she was on the phone to her surgeon in South Africa planning on having some of her lower ribs removed so she'd look much better in high-waisted trousers.

I straightened my hair with my GHDs and did my make-up and put on my new diamond dangly earrings that Wesley bought me which I'm terrified I'll lose one of 'cos they're proper expensive. Then I put on my new black dress from H&M that I'm proper in love with at the moment 'cos it just fits really well and it always makes me feel amazing. Then I put my Faith silver high heels on and spent twenty minutes trying to stuff my tiny handbag with my mobile phone, a cash card, housekeys, concealer, mascara, lipgloss and blusher. There's never enough room in a little bag. So I'm standing there wondering whether to give up and just carry a big handbag with almost my entire bedroom inside it, as usual, and that's when I heard the sound of a car outside the house. My lift had arrived!

I felt proper giddy then 'cos I'd been looking forward to this all day. I bounced down the stairs and chucked open the front door and there she was standing on the front door step.

'Uma!' I squeaked. 'Aight, bruv?'

'Shiraz Bailey Wood.' Uma smiled as she stood there in her skin-tight black denims tucked into black boots with fur trim, a black quilted jacket and her hair all scraped back off her face with big gold hoops on. Uma looked fierce as ever. She turned round and set the car alarm on the silver BMW X5 that was parked outside the house.

'OH MY DAYZ! Bare nang wheels, Uma,' I said.

'Innit, blud,' she said, laughing. Then she grabbed me and gave me a big hug. Uma smelled of Vera Wang Princess perfume and Nicorette chewing gum.

' 'Ere, shall I go and pay my dues to Mrs W?' she says.

'Oh go on,' I says, 'it'll make her happy. She's a bit of a misery this evening. She says the New Year can start without her.'

'What's up with her?' said Uma.

'Oh she's got one of her illnesses again,' I said, rolling my eyes.

So Uma wanders into the living room where my mother was sitting soaking her feet in a washing-up bowl and grumbling about a pain in her side that she's been wittering on about for days which comes on every time she needs me to put the kettle on and make her a cup of tea.

My mother's face lit up when she saw Uma, though.

'Ooh, it's you Uma! 'Ere, darling, how you been

keeping? How's your Zeus doing?' she said.

'Oh I'm good Mrs W!' says Uma. 'And Zeus is good too. He's really well in fact. He's in the bad books at the moment though. He ate a chair last week. Well not all of it, just both the arms and half the stuffing.'

'Oh my life,' said my mother. 'That ain't good.'

'No,' laughed Uma. 'My friend Aaliyah who I live with weren't very pleased, 'cos it was her chair.'

It's proper funny seeing my mother look all happy to see Uma 'cos there was a time when Uma weren't even allowed in the house. In fact there was a time when if Uma came to the front door my mother used to open it and slam it again and yell, 'Shiraz, will you tell that hooligan to stop making this end of the street look untidy. And tell her to stop coming to our door on scooters that ain't even hers!!!'

Uma went through a stage in Year Nine of riding little scooters around the estate that her brother Clinton had thieved. She'd ride them proper fast without a helmet on or nothing. I think she just liked the feeling of being free and on her own. Her house was always full of a right load of scumbags 'cos her stepdad was selling weed and the police were always kicking down the door, it was all quite heavy. This was all a long time ago. We've all grown up since then and lots of stuff has changed for the better.

'And your job's going well?' says my mother.

'Yeah, the casino is going really brilliantly,' said Uma.

'They've given me some wheels to get about in too. That's my motor out there. I love it.'

I went and checked out of the window to see if it was still there and no one was touching it.

'Shiraz is working down Lidl, did you know?' said my mother.

'Are you?' said Uma, looking at me. 'You never mentioned that, Shiz?'

'Yeah,' I said, feeling a bit hot all of a sudden. 'Yeah, I am, I thought I told you.'

'Nah, you never told me that,' said Uma, looking a bit confused. 'I'd have remembered that. How long for?'

'Erm . . . since about September or something?' I mumbled, looking at my fingernails.

'What happened to 118 118?' said Uma, 'You were working there in the summer weren't you?'

'Yeah I was there for a bit,' I said. 'But I left.'

'And now you're working at Lidl?' said Uma.

'Yeah,' I said.

'Full time?' said Uma.

'Yeah, full time,' I said, looking at my watch. 'Ooh is that how late it is!? Come on Uma, shall we head over to Carrie's?'

' 'Ere, Shiraz,' my mother said. 'Your Aunty Patricia was saying that she was in Lidl the week before Christmas 'cos they were doing Christmas crackers for one pound a box and she'd just seen it on *Lorraine Kelly Today*, but Pat said she couldn't find you there!'

'Well I was probably in the back, doing stock control and stuff!' I said, backing out of the door. 'I don't stand on the front door doing Meet and Greet. It ain't The Disney Store, Mother! Uma, I'll just get my coat.'

Me and Uma gave my mother New Year hugs and left the house and jumped into the 4x4. The seats were really soft plush leather. Then Uma switched on the seat warming pads so soon my butt was the toastiest thing ever. Uma's car has got an amazing stereo too. The speakers are proper surround sound and you can hear ever little beat and note of every track. Uma stuck on this really old Missy Elliot album called *Supa Dupa Fly* which she always used to be proper obsessed with when we were at Mayflower, then we set off down Thundersley Road, cruising towards the main road singing along to this track we both love called *The Rain* which has this amazing bit which goes:

Beep Beep
Who got da keys to tha' jeep?
VRROOOOM
I'm drivin to tha beach!

And we're both singing the *Vrooooom* bit well loud and getting all sorts of stares from gangs of boys at traffic lights in other cars which weren't as flash as Uma's, which was bare jokes. You feel proper safe in Uma's car 'cos you're sitting up high, above all the other traffic like you're in an army tank going to war or something.

'So how's life then Shizzlebizzle?' Uma says to me,

revving the accelerator as we waited for the lights to turn amber. Uma is such a girl racer sometimes, it creases me up.

'I'm good,' I said. 'It's all going OK. You know ... same old Goodmayes ting.'

'Yeah,' she says to me. 'And Lidl? What's that all about then?

'What do you mean?' I said. 'What's wrong with Lidl?' For a moment I thought she knew. But then I could see she obviously didn't. I was dying to blurt out what I was up to but I knew we only had about five minutes till we got to the party and to be quite honest I was scared she'd slip up and tell someone when we got there and it would all kick off. Not that Uma would do that. She's proper good with secrets. But I couldn't take the risk just then.

'Well, there's nothing wrong with Lidl,' said Uma. 'It's just that I just thought ... you know ... that you were going to try and do something a bit ...' Uma started to say something, then she stopped. 'What's the money like down there? Is it OK?' she said at last.

'Oh it's rubbish really,' I said. 'But Wesley spoils me, so I'm OK. I'm fine Uma honest, I am.'

Uma didn't say anything for a little bit, but you could almost hear all the words she wanted to say fighting in her head to get out,

'Yeah, but Shiz, you gotta start getting on track to earn yourself some proper money!' she said, sort of calmly but still a bit crossly. 'Don't be relying on a bloke for your money! Never. 'Cos I mean, your Wes is an angel, don't get me wrong, but blokes have a habit of being unreliable. You can't build your life around some bloke looking after you. You gotta have your own cash, like Beyonce says, innit? '*The shoes on my feet, the car I'm driving, the rocks I'm rocking, I depend on me!*'

'Yeah I know that, Uma,' I said.

'It's like all these WAGs you see, right?' Uma said, slamming on the indicator to drive up to the electric gates at Draperville. 'They don't have jobs do they? They just sit there looking vacant covered in fake tan and think that that some bloke will bankroll them, but then the bloke finds a new bird and they end up with nothing. No home, no cash, nothing. They've got brains the size of flies. Flipping WAGs? Pathetic they are.'

'Yeah, I know,' I giggled. Uma loves ranting about WAGs. We used to have to hide Carrie's copy of *Grazia* from her. She'd start flicking through it and spot a picture of Colleen McDonut or whatever she's called farting about the shops with her sunglasses on and then she'd just start ranting!

'I ain't like a WAG though am I?' I said to Uma.

'No, you're not,' she smiled. 'Not yet. 'Ere, don't start being like one or I'll have to come over and give you a slap.'

'Uma, stop being a rudegirl and park the bloody car, eh?' I said, laughing.

The security gates started to open and we both sat

mesmerized by Draperville for a few minutes. It was looking well festive in a proper surreal way as usual. The house was totally covered, every inch of it, in twinkling lights. This year Carrie's dad, Barney, had paid someone to climb up on to the roof and attach a sledge to the roof beside the chimney so it looked like Santa was just in the middle of delivering pressies! Then Barney had got someone to put a pair of false legs in red trousers with black boots poking out of the chimney, so it looked like Santa was stuck midway.

'Wow,' said Uma, 'It's just . . . Wow.'

'Big up Barney,' I said. 'He is such a big-in-the-Christmas-game kind of a geezer, innit?'

'Tru dat,' said Uma. 'That is well freaky though, isn't it? It's kind of scary to look at.'

'Yeah, he's had some complaints,' I nodded. 'There's a kid over on the Bovington Estate who got so traumatised by it Dr Gupta had to put him on Prozac.'

We drove through the gates and found a place to park. It looked like there was quite a lot of people there already. I hope they weren't all knobheads wrecking Carrie's parents' house. I like Carrie's dad.

'Anyway, that WAG thing I was saying,' said Uma, switching the engine off and looking at me. 'I'm not saying *you're* like that. I'm saying the total opposite. You've got a brain, Shiraz. A massive one. And believe me, bruv, that's a surprise to all of us to be honest, 'cos you've always looked a bit simple like you should be in your house crayoning something.' Uma looked at me with a proper straight face, then we both cracked up laughing.

'Cheeky cow,' I said.

' 'Ere, what's your Lidl uniform like?!' she said to me.

'Aw man, it is well bootilicious,' I said. 'It's a mauve coloured baggy shirt and some navy-coloured man's trousers. And a bright yellow name badge with Shareen on it. The name-badge making gun has broken so they're making me use an ex-member of staff's name instead. I was gonna wear the shirt tonight but I thought I'd best not. 'Cos I get some crazy attention from man dem when I wear it, they're throwing me their phone digits like crazy.'

Uma was roaring with laughter then.

'Look,' I said, being serious for a second. 'I've got a plan Uma. Don't fret about me. All this Lidl thing. I know what I'm doing. I'll tell you everything soon. I promise.'

'Oh . . .' said Uma, narrowing her eyes a bit. 'OK, hang on, there's something more going on to this than meets the eye, ain't there?'

'Yeah,' I said. 'Come on though, we gotta go inside. I'll tell you soon. All in good time.'

'Oh Shiz, but this is proper exciting!' gasped Uma, 'Oh I'm gasping for a fag now. 'Ere, wait on, I need to give my Nicorette patches a rub.'

'You serious about giving up the fags this time?' I said.

'Yeah,' says Uma. 'Aaliyah don't like me smoking in the flat so she's proper nagging me about it.'

'Ere,' I said. 'When am I going to meet this Aaliyah girl you live with now?'

'Ooh . . .' said Uma, then she thought for a moment. 'All in good time.'

We walked into the party and the first thing I thought was, 'Oh my God, who are all these randoms!?' The place was packed with girls and blokes I'd either never met or only recognised from Carrie's Bebo or Facebook. Even if they were all being well behaved it still looked like Carrie had just done a group shout out to everyone she knew from the internet and told them there was a party, which is a totally stupid thing to do but, let's face it, compared to other solid gold stupid stuff Carrie has done in the past would be actually quite tame.

Then I saw Collette Brown and the girls from Tanorife Vertical Tanning on the high street all standing over by Barney Draper's bar looking very, very orange with incredibly white teeth. Collette waved and said hello. It felt good to see her actually. I like Collette. Tanorife closed down for a while earlier last year when Collette's boyfriend went to prison, but she's split up from him now and opened Tanorife again. Apparently business has been booming ever since they won the *Now* magazine beauty award for doing the brownest fake tans in South East England.

Over in the corner I spotted some of the girls that Carrie used to go Butterz Beauty Academy in London with. They were all stood there with their long peroxide hair extensions, wearing tiny little dresses stuck on with tit tape and high heels. They all looked a bit like babes from a hip hop video.

I looked closer and I saw Wesley Barrington Bains II and Bezzie Kelleher stood behind giving out shots of tequila. Bezzie looked well drunk already. He was shouting to the DJ to put on some R&B and dance hall for the ladies 'cos it was New Year's Eve and this weren't the time to be busting out all the obscure drum 'n' bass. 'This is a party!' he kept shouting again and again.

Then Carrie appeared, looking really curvy and sexy, with her hair all in ringlets and wearing a navy blue baby doll dress with a low cut front which showed about as much of her boobs as she could get away with without the police being called for indecency.

A lot of the weight Cazza has put on has gone straight on to her scones and I didn't see any of the boys at the party complaining!

I felt like doing that joke my dad always does if a woman comes on telly with no top on. He always shouts 'Blimey madam, if you're selling those puppies I'll take the one with the pinkest nose!' This has been making me laugh for years and it ain't going to stop anytime soon.

'Shizzle! Uma!' shouted Carrie, 'Happy New Year's Eve!'

'Hello darling!' said Uma, giving Carrie a hug.

I was a bit distracted by what my Wes was doing to be honest. He'd given me a wave and a big smile when I got there and then made a face as if to say 'I'm coming over in a second', but he was having his ear talked off by this bird sitting at the bar with short black hair cut into a cute elfin cut wearing a tiny little silver skirt. And I mean TINY. So tiny I could almost see the gusset on her thong every time she crossed and uncrossed her legs! I watched him chatting to her and I felt a bit narked. Then I realised I was being one of them nightmare birds who you always see shouting at their boyfriends on a Saturday night so I decided to stop being a prat.

' 'Ere darling, you look gorgeous, why you so late innit?' Wes says to me, coming over as soon as he could get away. He seemed fairly 'well-oiled' too as my mother always says when she means drunk. But in a nice way. Wes is never ever lairy.

'Oh, I was faffing about getting ready babe, sorry,' I says to him. 'Who's that anyway? That bird in the silver skirt?

'Oh it's Carly Carrington, innit? You know?' he said. 'Remember Bizzy who you went to school with? That's his little sister!'

'THAT is Carly Carrington!' I said. 'It can't be! Carly's only a little girl!'

'She was a little girl back then, Shiz. She's seventeen now! She works at Tanorife.'

'Oh my dayz,' I said, staring at her. Last time I saw Carly she was running about Bizzy's garden with her Bratz dolls.

' 'Ere Shiz,' said Wesley. 'Carly has just let slip that Collette Brown is thinking of opening up two more Tanorife salons in Romford and Dagenham. And they're all going to need kitting out. New shower rooms and everything, innit.'

'Oh right! You gonna tell your boss about it?' I said.

'No,' Wes says. 'I'm gonna see if I can get the contract myself, innit. I could do that job no bother, Shiz. I know some good lads who do tiles too, innit. Teddy who I was at college with. He's doing well for himself now, innit. He's been doing 'wet rooms' innit. Like those posh people over in Wanstead have in their houses. I reckon this could be the year that Wesley Barrington Bains II makes some proper money innit?'

'You already make proper money, you plum,' I laughed.

'Well I do OK,' he said. 'But I want to start up on my own. Barrington Bains Plumbing, innit.'

I put my arms round Wes and kissed him on the lips. I know for a fact Wes could do this. Whatever my Wes does, it'll always be a success 'cos he's a really good plumber and he's true to his word and he always does his best. That's why people always call on him in an emergency. 'Cos he turns up when he says he will and saves people from a right load of misery. He's a star. I wrapped my arms round his waist and looked over my shoulder to make sure that that Carly Carrington could see that he was taken. She caught my eye and then looked away, looking well shady. She looked proper tipsy to be honest. So did everyone in the room. Well, aside from me and Uma who was driving so she didn't touch a drop. I took a few shots of something minging that tasted a bit like burned bananas, just to catch up, but shots just make me feel sick and dizzy. The fact is I am a legendary lightweight and I don't care who knows it.

As it got closer to midnight, the party was starting to get really mental and everyone was dancing and the Tanorife girls had climbed up on top of Carrie's dad's bar and kicked their shoes off and were doing lap-dancing manoeuvres and some boys Carrie knew from Ilford were sliding down the bannisters and Bezzie was hogging the microphone all to himself and toasting over the tracks, which sounds quite good if you've had a drink believe it or not. And I kept saying to Carrie, 'Oi, aren't you worried about the mess?' But Carrie kept saying, 'No, don't worry, I've asked Mrs Raziq to come in tomorrow and help tidy up.' And I kept thinking, Oh my dayz, Mrs Raziq is about sixty years old and only has one good eye! I bet I get a phone-call and get told to bring some bin-liners and dusters.

And as the clock crept up to midnight my Wes was clearly proper wasted 'cos he was being all daft showing everyone he could moonwalk to this old song by Michael Jackson called *Billy Jean*.

Of course, Wes can't moonwalk at all that's the funny bit 'cos he does it like your embarrassing uncle would do at a party, but that's the funny thing. So everyone was cheering and laughing and I felt proper proud to be with him to be honest, 'cos everyone loves my Wes and he even looked sexy when he was acting like a nork.

Then it turned midnight and everything went MAD and people were shouting and hugging and kissing and falling over. This is when Wes grabbed my hand and pulled me away from the crowd and into the garden. It was freezing cold outside now. Proper Baltic weather.

But we knew that Carrie's folk have got a little heater in the pool cabana area so we wandered over there and went inside and switched it on.

'I love you baby, Shizzle, you know that, innit. I love you to bits,' Wes said to me. Then he hiccuped loudly.

'Yeah, 'course I know that,' I said to him. We both sat down on the little bench. 'I never think you don't. I always know that.'

'You make me the happiest bloke ever, innit. ShishamBaileyshWood, innit,' he said.

'Yeah, you make me happy too, you donut,' I said.

'Do you remember the first time you came to my house that Saturday? When Carrie fancied Bezzie and we all went for a drive? And then she chucked us out of the car? We watched Channel U, innit?' he said.

'Ha ha, yeah,' I laughed. 'I was being proper cheeky to you wasn't I?' I said.

'You're always cheeky to me, innit. You're a right gobby mare, innit,' he said, squeezing my hand. Then we sat for a bit letting ourselves warm up in the heater. 'I loved you even then,' he went on. 'Right from the momentsh you came round my house that day, innit.'

I smiled at him and squeezed his hand back. Fair play, the alcohol fumes pouring out of his mouth were spoiling his romantic speech just a bit, but it was lovely all the same.

'And we're going to be together forever and get married and have kidsh and all zat Shizzle, innit?'

I thought for a bit when he said that.

'Yeah,' I said quietly.

'Thing is Shizz,' he said. 'You don't need to work down Lidl, innit. I know you say you like doing it, but you don't! Stuck in that stockroom all the time! They never even let you out in the main store, innit,' he said. 'When I get my business up and running, well, we could get married, innit. And you'd move into mine! And we can start a family. You could stay at home and be a mum, innit. Look after our little boy! Wesley Barrington Bains III innit!'

I looked at him and didn't say anything.

'I love you, Shirash,' he said. 'You're my woman, innit.'

'I think you've had too much to drink Wes,' I said to him.

'Yesh, maybeesh, hic,' Wes said. 'But I mean all of this, innit.'

'Yeah I know,' I whispered.

'So you want that too, promise innit,' he said, looking straight at me.

' 'Course I do, yes, I promise,' I said.

This is exactly what I said. I remember it coming out of my mouth. ' 'Course, I do. Yes, I promise.'

'Amazing,' he said. 'Big up me and you forever then, innit?'

'Yep, big up us,' I said and then he gave me a kiss. And then he put his head on my lap and fell fast asleep and started snoring. So I got my phone out of my bag and called Uma and she walked over the the pool cabana and started laughing and said, 'Oh dear. Shall we take him home then? I think the party's over for Wesley.' We delivered Wes back to his flat, practically carrying him in, and then Uma drove me back home.

Uma slept down at her mother's last night. I asked her if she wasn't nervous leaving the BMW X5 out in the street in case it got robbed and she just sighed and said, 'No, not really Shiraz, the biggest car thieves in Goodmayes will be in the next bedroom to me, so as long as I sleep with one eye open I'll be sorted.'

So I came indoors and got a glass of milk and got into bed. Then Penny came and found me and curled up in a ball beside me under the covers. And I thought for a bit about everything that had just happened that night. When I was still a bit tipsy it didn't feel so bad, but now it's 7am and I am stone cold sober and I'm thinking OH MY DAYZ SHIRAZ YOU KNOBBER, what the hell have you done?

I got woken up at 6am this morning 'cos our Fin was standing up in a cot yelling one of his very favourite words at the moment: 'MAISY.'

Fin LOVES Maisy the Mouse and he wants to watch her DVD all the time. He is OBSESSED by her. Maisy is a mouse who lives in a house and she knocks about with a crocodile called Charley and an elephant called Eddy. Maisy's whole life is just one non-stop round of high-jinx and crazy capers and our Fin can't get enough of it.

I must have watched that *Good Morning Maisy* DVD about two hundred and fifty times. In fact one night before Christmas, I woke up screaming in a cold sweat 'cos I was dreaming I actually lived with Maisy which meant that me and Tallulah the Hen had to share bunkbeds and a make-up bag and she was poking her beak in my eye-shadow.

Oh my dayz that was well freaky. I ain't a big fan of poultry at the best of times, especially when it's helping its claws to my lipgloss. So anyway, Fin first started shouting at about four in the morning and I heard poor Cava-Sue get up a couple of times and try and reason with him that it was 'Still night-time when Mummies and Daddies shut their eyes and stay quiet.' But this only worked for a little while 'cos soon Fin was shouting again, making it pretty clear that in his opinion it was morning-time, the time when little boys watch Maisy and eat toast and shout and scream a bit. No wonder my sister always looks like she's just fought her way through Afghanistan. In the end I decided to just get up. It was an important day today so I didn't want to sleep too late anyhow.

I swung my legs out of bed, shuffled across the landing and pushed the door ajar to Cava-Sue and Lewis's room. Fin was stood up in his cot, wearing only a nappy and a massive grin.

'Hello you,' I said to Fin.

'Allo,' he said with a smile that went from one ear to the other. He makes my heart melt, he does. I love him to bits.

It's like I can feel all my hormones going all wibbly in my belly when I see him.

'Toast?' I said to Fin.

'Toat!' he shouted back. 'Maisy! Toat!'

'Toast and Maisie,' I said. 'But first let's get rid of that whiffy behind, eh? Shall we get a fresh bumbos?'

Cava-Sue opened one eye and whispered, 'Oh my life Shiraz, I love you, you're an angel. I am so tired. Just give me half an hour and I'll come down.'

I changed Fin and then carried him downstairs, sniffing the top of his head, which smelled like baby shampoo and milk and fresh skin and soft hair just like babies' heads do. Part of me, just for a second, thought about what Wes had said about me on New Year's Eve. About me and him having a baby. He's not said anything since, but he did say it.

Our own little baby. One that was a bit of me and a bit of him. A little boy. Wesley Barrington Bains III.

Maybe that would be good?

But then I stopped myself right there and remembered our Cava-Sue lying upstairs looking all knackered. And I thought about how much she used to love going to London to see Emo gigs and come home at 7am from night-clubs and how serious she used to be about politics and environmental stuff. And she still tries to be, I mean, she TALKS about it enough, but nowadays she's too tired to go on protest marches and write letters to MPs. And at work at the Environmental Department she keeps getting offered better jobs for more cash but she always has to say no 'cos it would mean even more hours at work away from Fin. So she says 'No, thank you' and then she stays in the same job and gets depressed when some right old numpty takes the good job instead.

Since Cava-Sue had Fin she ended up sort of stuck. I don't want to be stuck. I want to be free.

And now Cava-Sue's getting hassle off our mother and all her mates down at the Mums and Toddlers group that she should have ANOTHER baby soon! People keep telling her that if she don't pop another one out then Fin will be lonely and he won't learn 'how to socialise and share!' In fact just this morning I heard my mother quacking on that if Cava-Sue didn't have at least another TWO babies really quickly like my mum did when she was her age then Fin would probably turn out to be the 'local weirdo', just like that bloke called Gerald Pritchard who is always on the front of the *Ilford Bugle* who collects German Second World War army uniforms and is always getting lifted by the police for being 'a public nuisance'.

'Really, Mother?' Cava-Sue said, trying to feed Fin some porridge. 'So Fin's going to be the local nutter?!'

'Well all I'm saying,' said my mother, 'is that Gerald was an only child too! I'm just pointing that out!'

'Mother, my Fin is NOT going to turn out to be the local weirdo,' said Cava-Sue. 'He's got plenty of friends at play group!'

'Well, pardon me for having an opinion,' tutted my mother. 'And as for you Shiraz, well, if you don't get your skates on you won't have a family at all.'

'Mother,' I sighed, putting on my Lidl name badge. 'I'm only twenty! You hear of women having babies aged forty all the time.'

'Pghghghgh!' spluttered my mother. 'Well, cleverclogs, and what you don't hear about is those women whose tubes all packed up before then and they end up without kids and having to adopt a foreign from Vietnam or Africa!'

I looked at her and counted to ten slowly in my head. 'Well I'll just adopt a foreign then, I like foreign!' I said, then I put my big padded coat on over my Lidl uniform and left the house to put a stop to the conversation.

I walked down Thundersley Road to the bus-stop, then hopped on to a number 60 bus. The bus was totally ramjammed with kids going back to school after Christmas and commuters making their way to Goodmayes station so I had to stand up all the way hanging off a strap like a monkey in the zoo. My big, heavy bag was digging into my shoulder. Between stops, I closed my eyes and tried to imagine I was in Uma's BMW X5 with the arse-warming seats and the surround sound stereo blaring out. About ten minutes later the bus began to empty of all the kids in Mayflower uniforms, rushing to make it before the start of day bell. I jumped off with them and walked in the same direction until I was at the front gates of the school, Mayflower Academy. Or Superchav Academy as it's still known to some people in Essex which isn't exactly fair 'cos things have got a lot better for Mayflower over the last five years. In fact some of the kids have been getting some really good results and getting good jobs. They don't put that in the newspaper much though. That's not as interesting a story as the time, back in the day, Clinton Brunton-Fletcher got on the roof with an air-rifle and took shots at the teachers' cars.

I went through the gates and walked in the direction of the separate block on the side of the school called 'Mayflower Sixth Form Centre of Excellence'. There was a lot of kids a couple of years younger than me, hanging about on the grass outside smoking crafty cigarettes and chatting on their mobile phones. A couple of girls I know in Khimar headscarves, Raya and Zayba, were standing gossiping outside. As I walked up they both swung around and said, 'Shiraz, hey how's it going?!'

'Not too bad, girls,' I said. 'Time to get back to it, eh?' They both laughed and groaned.

Then I wandered in through the front doors of the sixth-form block and walked straight into the ladies' loos. I unbuttoned my coat and quickly changed out of my Lidl uniform and slid on my denims and a pink T-shirt and my navy blue hoodie. Then I zipped it up 'cos the building was freezing 'cos the central heating hadn't started working yet. I looked at myself in the mirror before I left the loos and I couldn't help but giggle.

This Secret Squirrel thing is a massive pain, but it's sort of hilarious too.

Then the 9am bell rang and suddenly all the corridors were packed full of faces so I grabbed some stuff from my locker and walked upstairs to Room 5.8. I pushed open the door and there she was, stood by the blackboard with her back to me, looking totally fierce and pretty glam too in a navy blue pin-striped trouser suit and her long hair in neat dreads and then swept up into a bun. She looked more like a superhero than a headmistress really. I'm so glad she's teaching sixth-form English this term. She's one of the biggest reasons I came back.

'Happy New Year, Ms B,' I said, walking in and putting my bag down.

'Ahhh! Happy New Year indeed, Shiraz Bailey Wood!' 'Ms Bracket smiled, swinging round to look at me. 'You're back! I'm glad to see you!'

'Of course I'm back,' I said, taking out my pens. 'I'm sitting my A2 exams in June. I need all the lessons I can get.'

'Well precisely,' said Ms Bracket.

All the other English A-level students were coming into the room now. Last September when I decided to come back to Mayflower for one year and finish my A-levels, I was scared I'd not know anyone. And I was scared they'd all be a bit weird, 'cos I'm older than most of them. But I don't feel like that at all now. Adu, Raya, Zayab, Chrissy, they're all proper friendly. They think it's funny that I did the AS levels, went on an adventure to London and Ibiza and did some stupid reality TV show, then came back.

'I must admit I was a bit worried over the Christmas break,' Ms Bracket said. 'That you might get talked out of carrying on with your studies, once you told your parents what you were doing. You were going to tell them over the holiday weren't you?'

I cringed a bit when she said that and examined my fingernails closely.

'Mmmm,' I mumbled. 'Yeah, about that, Miss B. The right time never really presented itself. They still think I'm full-time at Lidl. But I'm not, obviously. I do one day a week. I will tell them though. I know it needs doing. It's just . . . I'm searching for that perfect moment.'

I sat there for a second and imagined the scenario.

I've imagined it loads of times before. The one where I wait until Nan is just passing around the jug of gravy at Sunday lunch and everyone's going, 'Ooh, lovely roast spuds Nan. 'Ere, who wants my sprouts?'

And everything's all cosy and lovely-jubbly and then I cough a few times to clear my throat and clink my glass of Netto Orange squash with a fork and ask for silence. Then I announce to everyone that I'm planning to leave Essex, forever most probably, to do a BA Hons degree in English Literature at a university in another city or maybe another COUNTRY like Scotland or Wales. And that I know this is very upsetting but I want to do something remarkable with my life. So remarkable that in future years if you stick my name into that Wikipedia site on the internet then you'll discover this amazing list of stuff all about Shiraz Bailey Wood of Goodmayes including the time in 2041 when I invented the cure for the Airbound Killer Transvirus 'Clack Clack' Disease that saved millions of kids from a terrible coughing death.

PLUS the time I wrote that six-hundred-page murder mystery which won the Booker Prize for literature AND NOT FORGETTING the time I travelled to Malawi, built an AIDS orphanage with my bare hands then sailed home single-handed on a yacht made solely out of Magnum lolly-sticks.

I don't think my mother will like this one little bit. Neither will my Wesley. Neither will Carrie, or Nan or Fin or Penny. 'Cos they all want me to be in Essex with them and they'll miss me if I go. And I know that's just 'cos they love me and I love them all back, I really really do, but the thing I've learned over the last few years is that if you have a dream, like my dream to go to university, then you have to follow it whenever and however you can. And I don't want to sound all cheesy like those X-Factor contestants who can't flipping sing going, 'I wanna be a pop star. I want it one hundred and ten per cent.' 'Cos that's just something people say to get on telly. I mean this in a different way. I think if you know exactly what you'd like to do in your head, like be a doctor or a dress designer or a writer or plumber and you ignore it 'cos of what other people are telling you, well it don't just stop the feelings. It just keeps on going around in your brain forever doing your head in. It just keeps on nagging you like a little voice in your head. Quacking on every time you're in bed going to sleep, and every morning when you wake, and there's another day all stretched out in front of you needing to be filled up.

So I reckon what I have to do is listen to that voice telling me to study and try and get a good job, 'cos even when I woke up in Whitechapel in London and in San Antonio in Ibiza or at Tiffany Poole's house, it was still there telling me to bloody go back to school and read some more books and . . . Oh my dayz, listen to me?! That's well heavy innit. But it's the truth. You have to listen to what your heart is telling you and keep it real.

'Anyway, Shiraz,' said Ms Bracket. 'You're an adult

now, so legally, you can tell your parents as much or as little as you choose. Obviously it would be ideal if your family could support your decision, but I understand if you need to find the right moment to tell them. Just talk to me if you start having problems. You will won't you?'

'Thanks Ms B, course I will,' I said, starting to blush a tiny bit 'cos I knew people were listening.

'Right ladies and gentlemen!' Ms Bracket said in her loudest, most assertive voice. 'Mouths closed, eyes looking at me. I need to speak to everyone seriously for a few moments. Now, firstly, welcome back, I hope you all had a relaxing break. But not too relaxing because this is where the HARD WORK begins and I need you working at full speed right away. We've got five months until the exams. And yes, I know that seems like a long time. Let me tell you, IT IS NOT. We've got a lot to cram in.'

We all stared at Ms Bracket. No one said anything. Everyone looked quite scared.

'Now,' she continued. 'I've been looking through some of your work over the break and my main impression is that your knowledge is good but your essay-writing technique needs some serious attention! AND I MEAN SERIOUS!'

We all groaned a bit then. I know this is one of my weak spots. Getting everything in the right order in an essay and making it make sense is a big problem for me. I know what I want to say, but I tend to get a bit confused and add in all sorts of things that make no sense at all.

'A bit like a drunk person after six pints of cider trying to tell a story in a pub,' is the comment Ms Bracket wrote on my last essay about Shakespeare's *Hamlet*.

'I'm going to make it clear,' said Ms Bracket to all of us. 'There's no point in learning all this information if you can't express it in an essay with an introduction, a coherent argument and a conclusion all wrapped up in under forty-five minutes. No point at all. You might as well go and scream at the moon!'

Everyone looked well scared now, aside from Adu who started howling like a werewolf and made everyone giggle.

'Thank you Adu,' said Ms Bracket. 'OK, today we're going to re-remind ourselves about "What makes a structured essay". Also did anyone buy any of the books I suggested before the holidays?'

'Me,' I said putting my hand up. Then I looked around the class. Total silence. I was the only one. Everyone looked at me and started to groan.

'Trust you, Shiraz Bailey Wood, you total BOFFIN,' giggled Adu. I sat for a moment and couldn't help but giggle to myself. Boffin? It was the first time in my life I'd been called a boffin instead of a chav. It felt kind of amazing.

THURSDAY 10TH JANUARY

I worked at Lidl all day today. Lord God give me patience. I only do eight hours a week there, almost always on Thursdays 'cos that's my reading day from Sixth Form. I do it for a bit of extra money so I'm not just spending my savings on books and travel fares. And most of the time I don't mind it but, other times, OH MY DAYZ it feels like the longest eight hours in the world ever. Not that I mind a bit of hard work, I like moving the boxes around and tidying the shelves and even mopping up the spilled pickled eggs, ESPECIALLY if I get a go on that mobile floor-cleaning buggy with the mops on the front. It's proper exciting if there's no customers in 'cos you can get it going at about six miles per hour. Sometimes me and Mohammed who works in the freezer section get both of them out on separate aisles and do Lidl Grand Prix. No, it's not the work I mind at all, it's just some of the people. Some of them totally do my head right in. Like Sandra Baggins the deputy manager who I had a bit of a run-in with today. Sandra Baggins is this enormous woman, about six foot tall and really bulky from Braintree in Essex. She's worked at Lidl for nine years and she started out in pickle stacking the same as me, but she has 'worked her way up' as she tells everyone ten times a day.

Sandra Baggins has false teeth on her top set of teeth – she takes them out and puts them in a glass of water if she's having anything soft like Müller Rice for her lunch. And she's got a peroxide spiral perm and she smells of Lynx Africa deodorant. And YES I know that is totally a man's deodorant but Sandra wears it 'cos she 'likes the smell'. And she's always opening the packets of custard creams and nibbling on them, then blaming it on the poor African night cleaners and she's always bringing in photos of her chinchillas for us to look at. Yes, she keeps chinchillas! Six of them! And man they are well spooky little things, like big fluffy rats with almost human faces!

And Sandra says she lets them sleep with her in the bed 'cos they keep her warm. And then – after all this – she sits in the coffee room with the *Ilford Bugle* putting circles around the *Dial-a-Date* messages saying, 'Oh boo hoo I can't get myself a bloke, I wonder why?'

And the thing is, I wouldn't mind any of this really 'cos it ain't none of my business, but the one thing Sandra is supposed to be in charge of is making the rotas and making sure I get paid each week and she makes a right pig's arse of that. In fact we keep having the same conversation again and again like she's got a big hole in the back of her head that all the knowledge keeps falling out of.

So today I was stacking a shelf full of Lithuanian gherkins (thirty pence for a massive jar! WOOT WOOT bargain alert!) when Sandra shuffles up with her big feet which always remind me of clown's feet and she looks at her clipboard and says: 'Hello, erm, erm, erm . . . Sharon . . . ooh what is it? Oh don't tell me!'

'Shiraz,' I said.

'Don't tell me it . . . It's here on the tip of my tongue!' she said.

'I'm Shiraz Bailey Wood,' I said.

'No you're not!' she said. 'Shiraz works over in the Romford shop on cold meats.'

'Well that must be a different Shiraz then,' I said trying to mask a sigh. ' 'Cos I'm Shiraz and I work here. Hello!'

'Ooh hang on, then?' Sandra said looking at her rota and seeming a bit bewildered.

'That's me on the next page at the bottom,' I said, pointing at her clipboard. 'You put a neon highlighter through my name last week, remember, 'cos you couldn't find me then either?'

'Did I? Ooh my head!' Sandra said, 'I'm all over the place at the moment. One of my chinchillas, Elvira, the black one, she's just had babies! I'm up all night at the moment with them. Have you seen the pictures yet?!'

'Mmm,' I said. 'I was on my coffee break before when you put all the blinds down and did the slideshow.'

'Oh good! They're little smashers aren't they?!' she said.

'They're very, er, mumph, nice,' I mumbled.

'OK, Shiraz,' Sandra said. 'Now I've just made the rota

for next week. Ooh don't let me lose it as I've not photocopied it yet. OK . . . So you're working on Sunday aren't you?'

'No, Sandra,' I said, 'I work on Thursdays. One day a week. Every Thursday. We agreed.'

Sandra scrunched her face up and looked confused again,

'Ahhhhhh, yeah . . . Thursday . . . I remember something about that now. Oh that's a shame, I've got you down here for Sunday! And you wanted . . . Thursday?'

'Yes, Thursday,' I sighed, trying to stay positive.

'Oh that is funny!' Sandra muttered to herself. ' 'Cos I need extra people for next Thursday too! And I don't need you so much on Sunday.'

'Good,' I jumped in. 'Then I'll do next Thursday instead!'

'Ooh, sorry love, no can do,' said Sandra, shaking her head. 'The rota is made now, I can't change it.'

I stopped stacking the jars of gherkins and counted slowly to ten.

'But you made the rota Sandra,' I said, trying to be calm. 'And you're holding it now. And you're holding a pen. Why don't you just cross me off Sunday and put me on Thursday?'

Sandra looked at me like I was a bit simple. Then she patted my arm and said, ' 'Cos you're down on the rota for Sunday, petal. I can't change the rota 'cos it's just been made.'

See this is when I lost my calm a bit. Uma wouldn't be happy.

'But Sandra,' I said firmly. 'There isn't any other copies of it yet! You only need to cross that tick out there and write my name on there and job's a good one, bruv.'

Sandra stared at the rota for a bit, her lips moving like she was really thinking hard. There was a long pause.

'But Shiraz you're working on Sunday. It's on the rota,' she said, looking a bit confused. 'Now stop arguing with me, petal. They made me deputy manageress for a reason. It's 'cos I can deal with things like the rotas and erm, other stuff. I worked my way up from stacking shelves like you now! If you work hard for the next nine years you can make the rota too.'

And then she walked off back to the store cupboard where I know full well she had a box of Highland Shortbread on the go, 'cos I kept hearing the crunching and finding the piles of crumbs.

I will not be here in Lidl in nine years' time! I am passing those flipping exams!

TUESDAY 15TH JANUARY

7pm – It felt funny the other day when Ms Bracket called me an adult 'cos I don't really feel like one at all. Most of the time I still feel like a kid. In fact the only time I feel like I'm getting older is when I'm dealing with my mother. 'Cos there was a time when she was definitely 'the grown-up' and I was 'the kid' and that was that. Plain and simple. But now and then lately, my mother does silly stuff and I feel the adult telling her off or bossing her about. Like today's sort-of argument we had about the doctors. My mother will not go to see Dr Gupta about the pain in her side, even though she's had it for a month. Before Christmas she kept remarking about the pain all the time, 'cos it was a good way to get us to do her favours like iron her work skirt for her or run her a bath, but now she don't mention it at all. This is 'cos she knows me and Cava-Sue will nag her to get it checked out.

So when I saw Mum proper clutching her side tonight and let out a gasp, I sat down beside her on the sofa, just me and her, no one else in the room, and I took the remote control off her and paused *Emmerdale* on Sky[+] and I said, 'Right, Mother, what is going on with you and this pain?'

'What pain?' she said.

'You know what pain,' I said. 'The one in your side.'

'Oh, it's fine,' she said. 'It's nothing, Shiraz. It'll go. I've just picked up a bug. Put *Emmerdale* back on.'

Now this was sort of annoying, as well as being proper double standards, 'cos if this was ME with a pain in my side even just one day, well she'd have booked me in at Dr Gupta's for a full body scan and then told Cava-Sue, Ritu and Aunty Glo about it and soon they'd all be stood around me screaming, 'Where's the pain Shiraz!? Is it in your kidney? Or is it in your vagina?! Is it your monthly visitor Shiraz!? Have you had a period recently Shiraz? Or maybe you're constipated! Do you need a poo? When was your last poo? Are you weeing normally? What colour is it? Is the wee pale yellow or dark yellow? 'Ere, if it's dark yellow then you ain't drinking enough water! Murphy, bring Shiraz a glass of water and then get on with making that sign in neon paint for the front door so all the neighbours know that Shiraz has had her daily poo!'

It would be a bit like that anyway. Maybe not exactly, but I'm on the right lines.

But when it comes to my mother's health, it's a private matter.

'Does it hurt when you go for a wee?' I said.

'What?' she said.

I just sighed and stared at her.

'No it doesn't,' she said finally. 'It's fine.' I knew she was lying.

'Does it feel like a stitch? Like if you've been running?' I said.

My mother just stared at the TV.

'Mother!' I said and poked her on the knee with my finger.

'I don't know,' she said. 'I ain't been running since I was fourteen.' Then she looked a bit sheepish like she was expecting me to flip out.

'Mother, will you go and see Dr Gupta please,' I said firmly. 'Shall I make you an appointment tomorrow?'

'I don't need an appointment!' she said, laughing like I was being ridiculous. 'It's not hurting any more. I'm OK.'

I gave her back the remote control and then I went into the kitchen to do a bit of my deep breathing. The thing a lot of people don't realise about my mother, 'cos she's acts quite hard most of the time, is that she hates going to the doctors. She's scared stiff of them. I know that. And if she won't go, then I can't make her. What do I do? Knock her over the head and then bundle her into Wesley's car? I can't force her to do anything can I? She's a grown bloody adult! I just wish she'd act like that sometimes.

10pm – I am not speaking to my stupid mother, so I've been sitting here upstairs in my bedroom ever since reading *Tess of the D'Urbervilles*. It is not cheering me up. I've just got past the rape part and now I'm on the bit where Tess has had the baby and it's died within a week and she's just had to bury it in basically a swamp at the back of the graveyard with just some flowers stuck in an old marmalade jar to mark the grave and to be quite frank, Thomas Hardy bruv, if this is meant to be entertainment it sooo ain't 'cos I half feel like killing myself! All I'm saying is that this book BETTER have a happy ending.

THURSDAY 17TH JANUARY

Tess of the D'Urbervilles does NOT have a happy ending. Thomas Hardy is having a laugh with that one, bruv. It should have been called *Life is Crap. And Just When You Think It Can't Get Any Grimmer, They Execute You Then Chuck You in a Swamp. THE END.*

FRIDAY 18TH JANUARY

I phoned Dr Gupta's surgery today when I was in the sixth-form meeting room. I thought I'd take matters into my own hands. Be the 'master of my own destiny' like Ms Bracket always tells us to be. Or in this case the master of my mother's destiny. Flipping whole lot of good that did me. It was like smacking my head against a brick wall. Basically, I called Dawes Road surgery and they put me through to the main reception desk and I got this really annoying woman, who sounded like even from the second she picked up the phone that she didn't want to speak to me.

'Dawes Road Surgery,' she said. But it didn't sound like that, it sounded like 'Dowsrdsgry'.

'Hello, I'm Shiraz Bailey Wood,' I started. 'I was wondering if—'

'Date of birth?' she asked.

'Pardon?'

'Date of birth?' she asked again, like she had the

80

hump with me already.

It annoys me when people talk to other people like they're a bit of crap they just found on their shoe. I don't think there's any need. Why do grown-ups go on about kids being rude and then they're more rude than kids could ever be?

'Oh, this isn't about me, I'm calling about someone else . . .' I said, quickly. I felt like she was going to cut me off if I didn't speak fast. To be honest, I could have done with a bit of patience here 'cos just talking about my mum being ill was making me start to get a bit tearful. I know it's stupid.

'Well,' snapped the woman. 'If this is about signing a new patient up with the surgery, then our books are closed. We've no space. Phone Chipping Wood surgery . . .'

'Eh?' I said, 'I don't want to sign up anyone else for the surgery.'

'Well what do you want today then?' she said.

'I need to book an appointment for my mother? With Dr Gupta please?'

'Dr Gupta is in Sri Lanka until February,' she said. Then there was a silence.

'Oh,' I said.

Crap, I thought, Mum'll only ever see Dr Gupta. She's been seeing him for twenty-five years.

'Will she see the locum?' the woman said.

'Oh, you mean the stand-in doctor,' I said. 'Who is it?'

'He's just qualified,' she said. 'He's called Dr Pipcock.'

'Yes, yes she'll see the locum,' I said. I was lying now but I was trying to buy more time.

The truth was, there's no way my mother would agree to see someone she didn't know who had just qualified. She'd say she wasn't being a medical experiment for some kid in short pants. I can almost hear her saying it. My mother can be very predictable sometimes.

'When can she see Dr Pipcock?' I said. There was a long silence.

'I've got 3.25pm on Monday 4th February,' she said.

'That's in over two weeks' time!' I gasped.

'Look, do you want it or not, I have someone on the other line?' she said.

'Well have you any emergency appointments?' I said.

'Well is this an emergency?' she tutted. 'If it's an emergency go to A and E!'

'I don't know if it's an emergency yet,' I said. 'I don't know what's wrong with her. I think she'd rather see a doctor.'

'Well if it's an emergency and she wants to see Dr Pipcock, she should come to the surgery at 8am and we'll fit her in when we can. But it might be a wait of anything up to eight hours as it's first come first served. Goodbye.'

And then the phone went dead.

So I sat there for a bit, feeling a bit tearful, and tried to work out what to do. Basically my mother has already said she won't go to the doctor's. Now I've got to convince her to take a day off work to sit in a waiting room for eight hours to see a man called Dr Pipcock who she doesn't know. Or go to Accident and Emergency and wait for eight hours there with all the junkies and the drunks. She won't do that either. I might as well go and howl at the moon. I sat there feeling a bit sorry for myself. And a bit wound up about how the woman had talked to me. Then I started remembering what it was like when Tiffany Poole needed a doctor. Tiffany doesn't have to wait two weeks to get anything checked out. She'll just phone up her own personal doctor on his mobile phone and he'd drive out to her mansion RIGHT THEN and put her mind at rest that the new freckle on her wrist wasn't skin cancer and that her choking fit wasn't her having a violent and fatal allergic to wheat. (She wasn't by the way, she'd just eaten her Shreddies too quick and they'd gone down the wrong pipe. Silly mare.)

But then Tiffany is rich so she paid for it all. It cost Tiffany a bomb though. Thousands of quid a year! Then I thought about my seven grand's worth of university money sitting in the bank and I felt really bad. It will pay my tuition fees for a few years if I don't blow it.

Then I sat in the common room and listened to everyone chattering on about university application forms which we sent off last year and the offers they'd started getting back and the interviews they were starting to get invited to. I folded my arms around my knees and realised I didn't have a bloody clue what to do.

Today was a well hectic day. I am knackered. I had classes all morning and a mock English timed essay at 2pm and then I rushed home at 3.30 'cos I promised Cava-Sue I'd collect our Fin from Amy the child-minder round the corner. When Cava-Sue first left Fin with Amy she was scared little Fin would feel neglected so she used to go to work snivelling tears down her cheeks every day. But now Fin loves going to Amy's and he shouts her name all the time which you'd think would make Cava-Sue happier but it don't, it makes her snivel even more. Cava-Sue does a LOT of snivelling. She is the families biggest sniveller. In the world snivelling Olympics she would get gold no bother. 'He loves Amy more than loves me!' Cava-Sue moaned this morning.

I don't think this is true at all, although I will admit that when I got there tonight he'd just found a box of Whiskas cat biscuits and managed to pour the whole lot over his head and pour the rest on the floor and he looked like the happiest little lad in the world ever.

'Devil-child strikes again!' I said, then I helped Amy with the mess, and took him home.

I put Fin in his cot and he had a little nap then I popped down to the kitchen 'cos I was starving. Just then Ritu and Murph walked in the back door looking like a right pair of miseries. Murphy had his hood up indoors which was a bad sign.

'Oh my dayz,' I said. 'What's happened to you two?'

'Don't ask,' grumped Murph, opening the kitchen cupboard and pouring himself a big bowl of Aldi Chocobangbangs and then pouring Rubicon Mango juice over it, which is well disgusting but it's one of his favourite dinners.

'Well I *am* asking,' I said.

I knew he wanted me to ask.

'We been on the train to Home Office in London today,' said Ritu, 'to talk to them about me staying in country.'

'Oh my dayz, what did they say?!' I said.

'Well,' frowned Ritu, 'in general sense, they are saying, well . . .'

'They said GET STUFFED,' said Murph, crossly shovelling cereal into his gob.

'We tried to claim asylum for me today.' said Ritu. 'I tell them I am an asylum seeker so I have to stay in Essex!'

I looked at Ritu a bit funny when she said that. I know a bit about asylum seekers 'cos I used to work with some of them at Tilak's pakora factory. 'Asylum' means that you have to stay in Britain 'cos if you go home to your own country the people there will kill you. Like just say you ran away from the war in Somalia or Afghanistan and they make you go home, well they might as well be sending you back to your death. Claiming asylum is really heavy. As far as I know Ritu isn't in any danger if she goes back to Japan.

'Ritu,' I said. 'I don't think you can claim asylum from Japan. You ain't really in any danger if you go home. Didn't your dad ring up here last week and offer to buy you a new car and take you skiing if you got your butt home pronto?'

Ritu looked a bit upset when I said that and I felt bad 'cos Ritu is such a sweet thing most of the time that no-one would ever want to hurt her feelings.

'Yes, I know,' she said. 'My father be very calm about all this, but my mother will shout loud and go crazy insane when I get there! I have missed a whole year of university! She send me here for one year to live in London and make good contacts with royal family and maybe marry Prince Harry. Well I did not do that. I e-mail her picture of Murphy to show her my boyfriend and she says, 'He look like homeless person! Why his trousers all hang down? I can see his underpants and they need good wash!' Then she said she will strangle me when I get home.'

'I don't think she meant she'd really strangle you, Ritu,' I said squeezing her hand. 'Parents always say stuff like that. Our mother has been threatening to smack, strangle and wallop the living daylights out of us for years. She never has yet. It's just one of them parent things. They get really angry at us and they say the first thing that comes in their head. They don't mean it.'

Ritu didn't say anything. She went over and put the kettle on, nodding like she sort of knew I was right. Then

Murphy picked his bowl up and slurped the rest of his Sunny D and some of it dribbled down his T-shirt, then he sniffed really loudly and looked all serious.

'You ain't going home, Ritu!' said Murphy. 'We'll find a way to keep you here! I'm going to sort this out!'

'Do you think so Murphy?!' said Ritu,

'I know so! There must be ways! And until then, you just keep on hiding up in the attic if you hear a knock on the door and we'll tell anyone official-looking who comes to call that you were last seen heading towards Heathrow airport, holding a ticket to Osaka, saying something about how you couldn't wait to get into the Departure Lounge and get yourself one of them big Toblerones for the plane. Or somefink.'

'Yes,' said Ritu. 'This is what we do,'

'And don't worry about nothing Ritu, right?' he said, standing up and walking over to her. ' 'Cos I love you and I'll look after you!'

'Oh I love you too, Murphy!' she said, throwing her arms around him.

'And I'll love you for ever!' said Murphy,

'And I'll love you for ever too!' said Ritu, 'We have to stay together!'

Oh my dayz, I thought. I only came in here to get a Fruit Corner. Now I'm in bloody Romeo and Juliet.

'Alrighty then,' I said, backing out of the kitchen as they both snogged each other's faces off. 'I'll just be going now. Enough spit-swapping thank you.

GOODBYE.' Then I came up to my bedroom and read about thirty pages of *Far from the Madding Crowd* by Thomas Hardy which is actually proper good and full of quite happy people. No one's been executed or died of blood poisoning so far, so it's all HAPPY DAYS.

I've just laid here for a while tonight thinking about Murphy and Ritu and about him saying he'll do anything for her. That's a big thing to say, innit?

I don't know what Wes will say when he finds out the truth. When he finds out I'm studying and that I want to go and live in another city. Will he leave Essex and follow me? Would he be happy there? Do I want him to come anyway? What if I get accepted by a college in another country like Scotland? Wes is scared of Scottish people ever since the Scotland football team played at Wembley and loads of blokes came down and ran around Trafalgar Square wearing kilts and those little orange wigs that are stuck to Tartan hats. Wes thinks all Scottish people dress like that. I've told him they don't but it's no use.

Wes has never been outside of Essex much. He's been to Kent a few times for Car Cruises but it ain't the same thing.

The thing is, something a bit weird happened this morning. I got a letter from Manchester University. A letter asking me to go up and visit on April 15th and speak to a tutor about maybe starting in September. They offered me a place if my grades stay high.

MANCHESTER! Where *Coronation Street* is. In

the north of England. I'd sort of forgotten I'd applied to there.

Ms Bracket helped me fill out my university application form a few months ago and I've been sort of blanking it out since then 'cos I'm scared. I totally didn't think I'd get any offers. I decided to apply to study English Literature Bachelor of Arts at Manchester, Newcastle, Edinburgh, Liverpool and Oxford.

YES, OXFORD. OXFORD UNIVERSITY.

This was Ms Bracket's idea. She reckoned that my predicted grades are high (how the hell did that happen?) and there's no reason why someone like me shouldn't go to a good university. (Erm, 'cos I'm a chav, or so people reckon Miss B, you crazywoman.) She even made me sit a little test sheet that Oxford sends out just to prove you're even worthy to apply to go there. Ms Bracket reckons Oxford University even sometimes gives folk from poor backgrounds an extra chunk of money so they can actually eat and have a place to live during the three years. I think Ms Bracket must be tripping off her nut to be honest, but I said yes just to make her happy. And now a letter has arrived from Manchester. I have to go and see them in April. I'm going to blank it out again now. I can't handle it at all.

SATURDAY 26TH JANUARY

11pm – my bedroom.

OK, we have a problem here. A serious one. I really want to call Uma and tell her but I can't face it. I know what she'll tell me to do. Maybe if I just lie here in the dark for a bit something will come to me.

4am – Well, that didn't work. Oh God, what have I done.

SUNDAY 27TH JANUARY

OK right, so my Wes rang me up on Friday and he said, ' 'Ere Shiz darling, you still want to go out on Saturday like we planned, innit?'

'Yeah, 'course I do babe,' I said.

Then he said, 'OK, just checking. I'm going to take us somewhere special, 'cos you deserve it, innit.'

'Oh you're a sweetheart,' I said. 'But you don't need to. We can just go to Fat Sam's Diner like we said. I know you like the burgers there. It's not too bad if you get a table near the front 'cos the birthday party people don't chuck food as much around down there.'

'No,' he said. 'I'm going to book somewhere posh. 'Cos erm, you've been having all sorts of worry recently with your mother and that Sandra woman who keeps messing up your wages down Lidl, innit.'

'Ah don't worry about me,' I said. 'Ooh and to be

honest, My mother seems a bit better anyhow.'

'Yeah, your dad was saying that, innit,' said Wes.

Now, I thought that was a bit weird, 'cos Wes hadn't seen my dad for ages. As far as I knew anyway. Wes hadn't been in my house for about two weeks.

I suppose I should have said, 'Oi, when were you speaking to my dad, Wes?' But I didn't get time to 'cos Wes said, ' 'Ere, gotta go princess. I'm talking on my mobile and I'm in the van. I'm not on my hands-free, innit.'

'Where you off to?' I said.

'I'm going round to meet Teddy, that lad I went to tech college with,' he said. 'We've got a few jobs to talk about, innit. See ya Shizzle. Love ya.'

So I'm getting ready tonight and trying to work out what to put on and I haven't got a CLUE 'cos if we're going somewhere 'nice' I don't know how 'nice' he's meaning. I mean is he driving me to one of those weird country-side golf club bars that Carrie's mother and father always go to which is full of Essex folk all trying to talk posh and pretend they ain't from Essex? What do I wear to go there? My mother's cream suit she wears to christenings and a string of pearls? Maybe some nice American Tan tights? One of them fascinator things in my hair that's like a hat but it ain't 'cos it's just a hair grip and it makes you look like you've got feathers growing out of your hairdo?

Obviously, this wasn't being made any easier by my mother who kept appearing at my bedroom door like a pest saying, 'Shiraz! Are you ready yet? Wesley is coming round at 7.30pm! Time is getting on, you know? Your table is booked for 8.30pm!'

And I felt like shouting, ' 'Ere mother, do you want to get your beak out of my business?!' but I kept my temper 'cos she seemed in such a good mood for once. And at the same time Cava-Sue was rushing about trying to get Fin bathed and put to bed early and I'm saying to her, 'What's the rush Cava-Sue?'

'Oh, erm, nothing. No reason,' she said. 'I just fancied getting Fin settled down nice and early!' then she disappears again in a cloud of baby powder.

Then I heard the sound of Wesley's car arrive and the door slamming and I could hear him set the car alarm, then ring the front door bell. Right away there was a massive huge fuss and everyone was whooping and cheering as if Wes had just arrived on stage at Wembley Arena to present an MTV Award or something.

Well eventually, after about ten minutes of me GHDing my hair and deciding on a dress and finding some shoes that went with the dress and finding my other dangly earring (under the stairs in Penny's basket, PENNY BAD DOG!) I went down into the living room.

My whole family, Cava-Sue, Lewis, Murphy, Ritu, Mother and Father were all sat there. Wesley was stood by the mantelpiece. When I opened the door everyone's head swung around to look at me and they all grinned at once showing all their teeth like they'd all joined this amazing religious cult and were hoping I'd come on board too.

'Hello ... erm ... my entire family,' I said, feeling a bit weirded out by them. 'Aight Wes.'

'Oh, don't you look pretty,' said my mother looking all happy.

'Eh?' I said. My mother never says I look pretty. My mother usually just scans my appearance and then wrinkles her nose and announces that the back of my hair looks like a thorn bush or my lipgloss makes my mouth looks like I've had my head in a honey jar.

'Yeah,' agreed my dad. 'She looks like a proper lady.'

'Right, erm ... OK,' I said, starting to walk through into the kitchen. 'Wes, I'll just find my house keys, can we go please?'

'Oh, Shiraz hang on, innit,' said Wes. 'Come here. I need to say something to you.'

'Well say it here, you nork,' I said, opening the fridge door and taking out the milk carton then having a big slurp, then trying to get the lipstick mark off the rim, so Cava-Sue don't have a minor breakdown.

'Nah, come here, innit,' he said.

'Oh hang on then,' I muttered, wandering back into the lounge. Then Wesley did something really really freaky. He got down on one knee. I just stared at him.

'What you doing down there, you plonker?' I said. But

93

Wes just gazed at me with a weird look in his eyes. At this point I started wondering if someone had spiked my lunchtime Bombay Badboy Pot Noodle with some magic mushrooms.

'Wesley,' I said, 'stand up bruv, you're going to burn your shoe on the fire.'

'Shiraz,' he said. 'I've got something I've been wanting to ask you for a while, innit. Something really important. You know how much I love you and how much I want us to be together forever, innit. So I was wondering if you would do me the huge honour innit of, like, being my wife and that, innit?'

'What?' I said, staring at him down on the floor. Then I spotted the ring box which was sat open in his hand. It was a platinum band with a pretty big sparkling rock set in it.

'Will you marry me, Shiraz?' he said.

I stared at him, then I looked round the room at all of the faces of my family. My mother looked so happy and proud that I thought her head was literally going to go BANG and shoot off into the sky. My dad was wiping away a little tear, so was Ritu and Cava-Sue. Even Murphy looked moved.

I didn't say anything for a moment. I was totally shocked. Then I looked at his eyes staring at me. It was like time stood still for a second. The rest of my life was going to be decided in the next few words I said. Yes or No? Yes? No? Yes?

The thing was, I couldn't remember anyone ever saying 'No' to this question. I've seen it on telly loads of times and I ain't ever seen any girl ever say, 'No thanks bruv, jog on.' And here was my Wes, on his knee in front of me asking me and looking proper sure and my whole family looking like it was Number One in their Top Ten Moments of their lives EVER. So then it felt like the choice wasn't yes or no. I had to say what I did.

'Yes,' I said quietly.

'YES!' shouted everyone, jumping up.

'Aw . . . I love you baby, innit,' he said and slipped the ring on to my left-hand engagement ring finger. It was a little bit loose on my finger and it felt really heavy. Then he grabbed me and kissed me on the lips.

'Ooh, I think she's in shock!' said Cava-Sue.

'Murphy,' my mother shouted. 'Go and get that big bottle of Lambrini out of the fridge and those special Babycham glasses that I got from the car-boot sale! This is a Wood family celebration!'

I don't remember much else about the rest of Saturday evening. Only the first bit really. I'm in shock. I know I went out to have some dinner, to that quite posh place in Romford called The Hartford, but I can't really remember what I ate. I just kept on looking at my hand and it's got a big rock on it and I appear to be engaged. Engaged to be married. Oh my gosh. I've really done it now, haven't I?

FEBRUARY

SUNDAY 3RD FEBRUARY

Some bare good reasons to put to Wesley Barrington Bains II why me and him should have one of those 'really long engagements' that lasts at least a couple of years (or even more).

1. We need time to save up! And we're going to need bare cash bruv, what with it having always been MY LIFE LONG DREAM to have a massive expensive wedding, with at least six bridesmaids (Uma, Kez, Cazza, Cava-Sue, Sandra from work and Elvira her chinchilla) and I must have one of them big wedding frocks that makes you look like you're playing The Fairy Godmother down at Romford Pantomime and at least one thousand guests including relatives I ain't even heard of before who've flown in from Australia. And I simply MUST get married in Saint Paul's Cathedral like a Royal Princess would, and then have everyone transported in coaches to a marquee round the back of the Toby Jug in Ilford afterwards where everyone can have full carvery and jam roly poly with the jug of bottomless everlasting custard. Oh and I want a full classical orchestra and Mariah Carey to play when I'm walking up the aisle and Take That singing me back down

afterwards. Oh and I MUST float off in a hot air balloon afterwards. YES THIS IS MY DREAM. And I know it sounds a bit weird and like everything I've always said I hated, but this is what I need. Even if it takes YEARS AND YEARS.

2. We also can't get married until Wesley converts to my new religion which is Islam. Well it may be Islam. I haven't decided one hundred percent because first I need to read and digest The Holy Qu'ran. FROM START TO FINISH. And I don't think I can do this great book justice unless I read it in Arabic first. So I'll need to learn Arabic. I called my mate Nabila this morning and she reckons this might take at least six or seven years. AMAZING.

3. We can't get married until I tone up my whole body pre-wedding so I look in the most ripped shape I've ever looked in my life in my wedding dress for the big photo session. This will obviously involve me weight-training, long-distance running and swimming bloody miles every day. In fact I'll probably have to enter a few of those Iron Man competitions like you see on telly where you've gotta swim across the Thames, then run through London in a thong swimming cossie spending half the time retrieving it out of your doo-dah, then cycle the rest of the way and by the end of it you're fifty pounds lighter but you need to go in an oxygen tent. But imagine how good I'll look

afterwards in an off-the-shoulder bridal gown!!! YES THIS IS MY GOAL. This might take five years.

4. Also, I don't want to get married until me and Wes have mastered Irish Dancing 'cos it has long been my dream to have a full Irish dance troop perform at my wedding with me and my groom as the starring roles doing that weird 'arms clamped by your side/legs flinging about like a mentaloid' extra-fast dancing. Sadly, this might involve me going to Dublin for a long while and not coming back until I've learned all the complex fancy footsteps and spinning jumps that I've seen on my nan's *Shamus O Donnaghty: Feet O' Fire! DVD'* that she got free with *The Daily Mail* and watches six times a week.

And, 5. We can't get married for a long long time, 'cos I don't really want to get married. Maybe later, like in a few years' time or something 'cos I do think the world of him. But not now. (This excuse might take a bit of padding out and maybe a joke or two in it, 'cos it's gonna break my poor Wesley's heart.)

THURSDAY 14TH FEBRUARY

I got up this morning and went in the shower, then put on my super-hot bootilicious Lidl uniform. I was actually working at Lidl for real today, not faking for once.

Then Cava-Sue walked in carrying Fin in one arm,

who was waving about a piece of cardboard covered in glitter and bits of silver paper. I thought it was something he'd maybe made down playgroup. It had weird sticks stuck on the front.

'What's that he's got?' I said.

'It's a card to us from his dad,' Cava-Sue said.

That's when I remembered it was Valentine's Day. The Day of Love.

'Aw bless Lewis, look at it!' said Cava-Sue.

'To my girlfriend and our little boy – I love you both from Looooeyxxx,' it said on the front.

'Lewis knows I think cards are a waste of environmental resources. So he made this from stuff out of the re-cycling box,' said Cava-Sue. 'Look! That bit there is an old milk carton top! And those words there are made out of old chicken bones from last Sunday lunch!'

'Oh my God, is that what the smell is?' I said, taking a few steps back. Murphy had been sucking those bones!

'Eh?' she said.

'Oh, erm, nothing, I'm just saying it's lovely,' I said quickly. 'Really sweet.'

'Hey, hasn't your Wesley Barrington Bains II bought you anything? No card or nothing?!' smiled Cava-Sue. 'Oh what am I saying? Of course he has, he always does.'

'Nah, the post has just been and I've not seen anything,' I said. I turned my back to Cava-Sue and looked at the letter I'd just found on the mat addressed to me. It looked like a mobile phone bill or something. I quickly opened it and felt my knees go all wobbly. It was from Oxford University! They wanted me to go and see them on May 18th for a 'campus tour' and to discuss my future.

OH MY LIFE.

I looked at it again quickly and felt really sick. Then I stuck the letter in my pocket. It had to be a wind up? Oxford. Nah – no way. I decided then that I was going to ignore it.

I've seen Oxford University on the telly and I know it ain't a place for Shiraz Bailey Wood. Deep down, part of me thinks that no university really is, but definitely not there. Oxford is full of people called Farquar Fossington-Smythe and Amelia Posenby-Bumbogey and their dads all know the Prime Minister and they go to balls all the time and ride ponies to their lectures and shout 'A flagon of foaming ale, my good lord!' when they walk into the pub. It's not for me. No way.

Suddenly I realised Cava-Sue was talking to me.

'Where's your ring?'

'What ring?' I said to her.

'Your engagement ring, Shiz,' she said, rolling her eyes at me.

'Oh God,' I said. 'I took it off last night before bed. It must be upstairs. It feels really weird. I need to put it in the jewellers to get resized I think. It makes my hand feel . . . weighed down.'

Cava-Sue laughed when I said that.

'Well, you better get used to it,' she said. 'You'll be wearing it for ever. Hey and when you get the wedding ring you have to wear it on the same finger for ever too! For ever and ever!'

I wished she'd stop saying for ever. I wasn't in the mood to think about for ever.

'That's why the ring is such an interesting symbol of marriage,' said Cava-Sue buttering some toast and putting it in little pieces for Fin who was in his high chair. 'Because it's a circle. The circle symbolises eternity. 'Cos there's no end to it. It just goes on and on and on!' I looked at her and said nothing.

'Hey,' she said, 'I've got an interesting book somewhere in one of my crates in the loft. It's called *The Women's Room* by Marilyn French and it's about the frustration and resentment of living with men and how womankind can cope and still be independent! Do you want to borrow it?'

'Erm,' I muttered. ''Ere Fin, how about a bit of Maisy! Shall we watch a DVD before Aunty Shiz goes to work!?'

'MAISY! MAISY! MAISY!' shouted Fin. 'Come on then,' I said scooping him out of this chair and carrying him into the living room where my mother was sat in front of the TV in her dressing gown and slippers watching *GMTV*.

'MAISY,' shouted Fin.

'No, no Maisy just yet,' she said. 'Granny is watching this!'

'Hey I thought you were having a day off in bed?' I said to her. She's got a cold at the moment and it seems to have got into her lungs so she's been short of breath. But this wasn't bothering her right at this moment, 'cos on the screen there seemed to be some sort of feature going on about luxury weddings. There was images of fancy Rolls Royces and a model wearing a big white dress. Then a massive seven-tier wedding cake with a marzipan bride on the top. Then some shots of tiny little bridesmaids in expensive dresses that made them look like little princesses. Then a real New Orleans jazz band playing in a marquee while the bride and groom danced. It was a fairytale wedding. A bit like the ones you see in those magazines my mother has started bringing in the house recently called *Brides Now!* or *Your Big Day.*

'Oh, isn't that lovely Shiraz,' said my mother, pointing at the telly.

'What is this?' I said. 'Is it a competition or something?'

'Shhhhhh,' said my mother, putting her finger to her gob.

GMTV was back in the studio now, Darleen Young was on the couch.

'So now we've seen the amazing wedding on offer!' said Darleen, flashing teeth so white you can't actually look at them 'cos it makes your eyes go a bit wonky afterwards. 'This really is an incredible once-in-a-lifetime wedding on offer here, with a value of one hundred thousand pounds! And we've had so many couples entering our competition absolutely dying to win it. The on-line entries were flooding in right until the Valentine's Day cut-off point. And our judges have been here all night, reading every single one. But we've finally made a shortlist of four! Those four lucky couples will have a chance of winning that BIG DAY. And we'll be filming it all for *GMTV*!!'

'Mother will this go on for long?' I said. 'I promised Fin some Maisy before he goes to Amy's house?'

But my mother was right up at the telly with eyes almost as big as the screen.

'And the first couple to make the final are . . .' said Darleen, pausing to make it more exciting, 'Yolande Travis and Tevin Young from Birmingham!'

'Damn it,' muttered my mother.

I looked at her face, all disappointed, and I suddenly felt very cold. She wouldn't have. Would she?

'And the next couple are . . .' cried Darleen, 'Lisa-Jane Howard and Curtis Kelly from Sidcup!'

'Murphy!' yelled my mother, turning round and opening the lounge door to let her voice boom up the stairs, 'Are you sure that internet thing of ours is working?! It ain't on the blink again is it?'

'Mother!' I said, starting to raise my voice. 'You didn't by any chance enter me and Wesley into this competition?'

But my mother was pretending not to hear me.

'Couple number three are . . . Buttercup Bettany and

Jean-Claude Jones!' shouted Darleen Young.

' 'Cos if you have,' I said, 'I'll be really bloody livid, Mother. It's one thing buying all those magazines and folding down the pages on dresses you like ... and blackmailing me about having Aunty Glo's god-daughter as a bridesmaid when you know she wets herself all the time but—'

'Now this final one is a real mouthful!' said Darleen. 'Let me get this right ... the final couple with a chance of winning the wedding are ... Shiraz Bailey Wood and Wesley Barrington Bains II!'

'HOORAY!' screamed my mother, lifting off the sofa like a sky rocket then sitting back down clutching her side and coughing a load of phlegm up then waving her arms about like she was a backing dancer on *High School Musical*.

'Did you hear that Shiraz! You're in the final four! You could be having a luxury wedding this August!'

I sat back down on the chair and put my head in my hands.

Just then the front door bell rang. Cava-Sue answered it then wandered back into the living room carrying an enormous bunch of red roses. At least forty eight roses, it looked like.

' 'Ere Shiraz,' said Cava-Sue. 'It's from Wesley, I reckon. See, he did remember.'

'Yeah,' I said, 'Cheers sis. Nice one.'

Kezia and Carrie are VERY VERY excited about the *GMTV* wedding thing.

Kezia says, 'Oi Shizzam, will there be a free bar at your do if you win then? 'Cos I want to get proper steam boats! And what about karaoke too?'

'Dunno Kez,' I said.

' 'Ere, do you need security for the marquee?' Kez asked. ' 'Cos I was down at Rose's last night, 'cos she was minding Saxon and Rose's new bloke has got his own security firm?! He doing all the nightclub doors in Ilford now.'

'No I think I'm OK for security, Kez,' I said.

'Or fruit machines? Do you need any sort of gambling machines 'cos he hires them out too?'

'Nah, I'm good, Kez, honest,' I said.

' 'Ere Shiraz,' Carrie butted in quite crossly, taking a big piece of Mexican Meat feast pizza that Bezzie had biked round specially for our night in. 'Have you chosen your bridesmaids yet or what?!'

'Ooh erm ... No, not really thought about it,' I said to her.

'Well don't you think you better had, just in case you win, 'cos it'll be happening in a few months!'

They both stared at me really hard when Cazza said that.

'Look,' I said. 'I'm not going to win the competition. The other girls were like models and their fiancés were soldiers who'd been to Iraq and one of the girls had a heart defect and stuff like that. Proper sob stories. 'They'll win, not me. Me and Wes will need to save up. So I'm not getting wed for at least two years. Maybe a lot longer.'

Kez and Carrie looked proper devastated when I said that. I felt bad then.

'Hey, but . . . y' know, obviously, I would be honoured to have you both as my bridesmaids whenever I get wed,' I said. 'Cos obviously you're my girls, innit.'

'Would you?!' said Carrie. 'Amaaaaaaaaaaaazing!'

'Ha ha! Well we'd better both say yes then, bruv!' laughed Kezia. 'Oh this is well good isn't it? 'Ere, what about Uma though?'

'Yeah and Uma too,' I said. 'Of course Uma.'

'Oh my dayz!' said Kez. 'I can't wait to see Uma's face when she finds out! What a wedding this is going to be?!'

'Yep,' I said. 'It sure is.'

' 'Ere, I need a dress that covers my tattoos. I'm sick of some of them already. Why did you let me get that one done in Ibiza?'

'Yeah,' I sighed. 'I AM sorry about that, Kez. That was my fault, wasn't it. I shouldn't have forced you.'

'Oh God,' said Carrie. 'I have got to start on my diet again tomorrow! But until then, who wants some of this ice cream Bezzie brought us around. It's Chunky Monkey! 'Cos that's what he calls me, innit. His little chunky monkey!! Ain't that lovely eh! And I call him

Bezziebaby! Oh Shiraz, you're so lucky getting married! I'd love to be in your position right now. You're going to be a princess for a day!!'

'Yeah,' I said. 'I can't hardly believe what's happening myself.'

THURSDAY 28TH FEBRUARY

OK, today was a bit of a weird one. My head is in bits. I was at school in History when my mobile starts vibrating 'cos it's switched on to silent, and a 'Private number' flashes up. It rang and rang. So I thought, 'Well I'm not picking that up. I don't do private numbers.' So I flipped it on to silent and then watched as the number called again and again and again. So in the end I shoved the phone in my pocket and told Mr Higgins that I needed to use the bathroom quickly 'cos it started to make me think it was maybe serious.

As it rang for the fifth time, I picked it up and a woman's voice said, 'Is that you Shiraz? It's Hope. Hope who works with your mother.'

'Hello, Hope,' I said. Now this felt weird right away 'cos I've never spoken to Hope on the phone ever. In fact how did she have my number? 'What's up? Is everything OK?'

'Erm, not really Shiraz,' she said. 'Look I don't want to upset you but I've just put your mum in an ambulance to hospital. She's gone to Whipps Cross A and E.'

'Why?!' I said.

'Look, me and Josie went off on lunch together 'cos the bookies was quiet,' she said. 'And your mother was here by herself doing the counter. And you know she's had that cold and she's been puffing and panting a bit? Well she seemed a bit worse today so we said we'd fetch her some more medicine from Boots. But when we got back . . . well we couldn't see her . . . and she was like, well, lying behind the counter. Like she was . . . well, erm, well she didn't look good.'

'What do you mean?!' I said. 'Had she fainted?'

'We don't know, Shiraz,' said Hope. 'She was just lying there. We tried to bring her round, but she was, erm, pretty much out cold. Oh Shiraz, I don't want to scare you . . . it could be nothing . . . it could just be nothing.'

My heart was banging at about one hundred miles per hour in my chest now.

'It didn't seem like nothing though did it?' I said. My voice was going all wobbly. 'Oh God, OK. I'll get to the hospital now. Does anyone else know yet?!'

'Yours was the only number we could find,' she said. 'She's got it written on a sticker beside her phone. Are you OK to call other people Shiraz? Are you OK to go to the hospital?'

'Yeah . . . yeah . . . I'll set off now . . . thanks Hope . . . I gotta go, thank you. Thank you for calling the ambulance, thanks, I mean . . .' I was trying to finish the sentence, but I had to hang up, 'cos I was starting

111

to cry. Then I stopped myself and told myself to get a flipping grip.

It was one of them situations again where I was going to have to be a grown-up and work out what to do. My dad would go to pieces when I told him, so he'd be no use. He's crap in emergencies. I also knew Cava-Sue would definitely get in a flap about how there was no one to pick up Fin and give him his dinner and put him to bed 'cos Lewis was working late tonight. And Murphy is still the baby of the family so no one asks him to do anything. The fact was that I needed to take charge of all of this and go and find my mother and talk to the doctors and work out how to make her better again and do all the stuff like a grown-up would. I sat down on the little bench near the teachers' car park and let myself have a few little tears and then I picked up my mobile and called the one person I know who is basically a kid like me, but who can be a grown-up when he needs to be. His phone only rang twice and then he picked up, and I told him about my mum.

'OK, no worries princess,' Wesley Barrington Bains II said. 'You head towards the hospital, I'll meet you there as soon as I can. I'll finish this job I'm doing early and come now. Hey and don't panic, innit. It's all going to be fine, innit.'

When I got to Whipps Cross I ran into A and E and asked for Diane Wood but they said that she wasn't with them any more 'cos she'd been moved up into the intensive care unit. The nurse said they wanted to keep a proper eye on her because she was in a bad state.

'Why?!' I said, but they didn't seem to know. They just said that my mother was 'very poorly' and they had to run some tests. So I set off to try and find the Intensive Care unit but the hospital started to feel like a maze then. I started going upstairs and back down other ones and soon I was totally, utterly lost. Apparently the place I needed was on floor five in the green quadrant beside the Brook Green ward, but the more I looked at the map the more I felt like sobbing. Then a boy's voice said to me:

'Can I help you at all, are you lost?'

I turned round and there was a young guy who seemed to be a doctor standing there. He looked about the same age as Cava-Sue, with pale brown skin and a white doctor's coat on.

'Do you know where Intensive Care is?' I said.

'Yes, I'm just going there now. Come with me, you're not that far away,' he said. He had quite a posh accent.

I felt like hugging him when he said that, 'cos he had big kind brown eyes and was the first person who'd been helpful since I'd got there.

He walked through the doors of Intensive Care with me and then disappeared off into another room, leaving me to tell the nurse in charge who I was.

'OK, Miss Wood,' she said. 'Well I've not got a lot of definite news about your mum I'm afraid. She's very weak and she's been in and out of consciousness a few times since she arrived. She's got severe pain down the right side of her body, around her lungs, in her kidney and all over her back. Is she under any treatment for anything?'

'No . . .' I said. 'She's been saying she had a pain in her side for a while . . . but . . .' I felt terrible then. Why didn't I put my bloody foot down about seeing her doctor? I've been so busy studying for these exams and worrying about the wedding thing that I totally let my own mother down. I AM THE WORST DAUGHTER EVER. 'Can I see her?' I said.

'Just for a few minutes,' said the nurse. 'She's just over here.'

I followed the nurse down a little side corridor and into a tiny room which was really quite dark.

And that's where she was. My mum. Lying in a hospital bed looking . . . well pretty much like a dead person really. I knew she wasn't though, 'cos there was a machine beeping beside her. I don't know what the machine was for but I've watched enough episodes of *Holby* to know that if the machine is still beeping that it's GOOD NEWS. It's when it suddenly goes 'Durrrrrrrrrrrrrrrrrrrrrrrrrrrrr' that you need to start worrying. At the moment there was still a regular beep and I was really glad to hear it.

Mum's skin was really pale. Pure white almost. Her eyes were closed and I could see tiny blue veins in her eyelids. Her blonde eyelashes fluttered as she breathed. Her eyelashes were actually a little bit ginger now that I was right up close to them. I'd not noticed that before. Or if I had, I'd forgotten. When I was a tiny little girl I used to sit on top of my mother all the time when she was trying to watch *EastEnders* or read a magazine and I'd jump on her knee and cuddle right up into her face and pull her hair and go to sleep with my face in her neck. Or I'd point at bits of her face and go 'Eye!' 'Nose!' 'Ear!' and she'd say them back to me and then she'd blow a funny noise on my head with her lips and we'd both laugh and laugh for ages.

But then I got bigger and we stopped having many cuddles. I was too old for cuddles. She'd take me to the gates of the school when I was like seven or something and say, 'Right Shiraz, I'll be back later,' and lean down to give me a kiss, and I'd go 'Gerrrrrrrroff,' and walk off wiping my cheek to get her lipstick off. My mother would just roll her eyes and walk in the other direction, usually not even looking back. It was like the battle of who was least bothered and she often won. I didn't need her fussing me any more. If Uma and Carrie weren't getting kisses off their mums any more then I wasn't either!

So anyway, sometime about twelve years ago I sort of packed in kissing her and she stopped kissing me and it was an agreement we were both happy to live with. Until now. I stared at her lying there with a little mask over her mouth which was helping her breathe and a tube stuck her arm attached to a weird plastic bag of gunk. Then I leaned over the bars of the bed and kissed her forehead. My mother was totally out cold. There was no way she could see or hear me. She was in another place completely.

'We've made her as comfortable as possible,' said the nurse. 'But we're waiting for the doctor to do his rounds before we can give you any more information.'

'OK,' I said.

The nurse walked off and left us alone.

'Oh my days, Mother,' I whispered. 'What the heck has happened to you?!'

She didn't have many answers though. She just lay there. It was probably the quietest I'd seen my mother ever. EVER. And right at that moment I'd have given ANYTHING IN THE WORLD for her to sit up and go, ' 'Ere Shiraz, what's going on with your hair? Why do you come up to Intensive Care looking like a homeless person. Can't you at least stick a comb through the back of it, or is that the 'fashion' nowdays!?'

I pulled up the chair beside the bed and sat there for a while staring at my little poorly mother in total disbelief.

Then the nurse walked back in carrying some files and put one at the end of my mother's bed.

'She's not, like, dying is she?' I said.

My stomach went all wonky as I said the word dying. I was really hoping that the nurse would say, 'No, no, don't be silly. That won't happen.' But she didn't, she just said, 'As I say, the doctor will be able to tell us more.' And then she made me go and sit in a chair in the family room where I sat waiting for hours and hours.

Next to arrive on the scene was Wes, then my dad, then Cava-Sue who started getting really bolshi with the nurses and asking tonnes of questions, which they didn't know the answers to. This only made us all feel worse, but I didn't have the energy to tell her to shut up.

'Could she die?!' Cava-Sue was saying. 'We need to be prepared for the worst!'

Well, I didn't agree with Cava-Sue about that, 'cos if my mother was going to breathe her last tonight, I'd rather it was sort of sprung on me in about six hours' time and I could deal with my life being destroyed just then. At that point I was still trying to cling to this thought that she was just having a lovely lie down and at any moment would sit bolt upright in bed and say, 'What are you lot all bloody doing here? Can I not get five minutes' peace? Did anyone let Penny out for a widdle before they left? Oh typical, I have to remember EVERYTHING.'

Later on, when Cava-Sue started kicking off at the doctor with the brown skin and the nice eyes he stayed very calm and tried to help her.

'If this is a serious renal problem then, yes, things might be very tricky for your mother and it could prove fatal,' he said. 'But it's far too early to know now. In fact we'll be running tests for days. I'd suggest that you go home and get some rest. She's in a stable condition at the moment.'

'What does that mean? Where are your renals?' my dad said. I could tell he'd been crying and it was making me scared. I have only ever seen my dad cry once, when his mate Lazza, who he always went down Goodmayes Social with, got squashed by a truck, and that was fifteen years ago.

'It's your kidneys, Dad,' I whispered.

'Oh God,' he said, then he went really quiet. Then we all sat and said nothing for a long time and the clock on the wall ticked very slowly and nurses came and went but didn't meet our eyes when we looked at them 'cos they didn't want to get dragged into our questions. And in the middle of all this my Wes was busy, going to the vending machine and getting coffees and KitKats and phoning Lewis to give him messages from Cava-Sue, then phoning my Aunt Glo to say Mum wouldn't be down Mecca Bingo tonight or any night for that matter for a long time, then offering to drive people home or go and fetch mum's stuff from the house and bring it back to the hospital.

My Wes is a star in emergencies. He's what older people would call 'a godsend'.

MARCH

FRIDAY 7TH MARCH

It's been a horrible week. I'm sick of the sight of that hospital. And the smell of it is on all my clothes and in my hair. The one thing we know for sure now is that the reason my mother's got all sorts of nasty pains in her lungs and back is 'cos she's got this thing called pleurisy. She's not in intensive care any more, she's in another ward. We're allowed to visit for an hour at lunchtime and an hour at night. I've been going every night. I don't really understand what pleurisy is, but it's like an infection and she's got like the worst kind of it ever. She can't move out of bed and she can hardly even speak. The thing the doctors don't seem to know is why she's got the pleurisy and why she keeps getting worse instead of better, no matter how much gunk they drip into her arm or special beeping machines they stick beside her bed. This is the thing that is scaring me. Why is it not getting better? I'm not telling anyone in the family how scared I am 'cos it will make everyone else freak out too.

They've been doing all sorts of tests on my mother's heart and kidneys and liver but they don't seem to ever say for straight that she's going to get better. They just keep asking for more time and saying that she's as comfortable as possible and we should try not to worry. They say they want her to stay in hospital. That's fine by me. It's not like me and Cava-Sue are going to sling her over our shoulder and carry her out going, 'Sorry bruv, jog on, we're taking her down Jumping Jacks at Romford for two-for-one cocktails.'

Cava-Sue is doing my head in big time right now. I know she's trying to make things better and I'm an evil cow for saying this but she's making things worse. She turns up at the hospital every flipping day with printed-off sheets from the internet, full of stuff she's read on health messageboards and it is all HORRIBLE and DEPRESSING. It's just sheets and sheets of random strangers, saying stuff like, 'Ooh my friend had pains in her lungs and her kidneys and then guess what. . . . SHE DIED IN HIDEOUS PAIN INVOLVING A POINT WHEN ONLY GREEN GOO SPURTED OUT OF HER MOUTH AND EARS! Ooh terrible it was!'

And then someone else will chip in, 'Pains in your back and kidneys? Oh yes that's the first sign of lung cancer! Don't listen to those doctors they know NOTHING! You'd be better off not being in hospital at all! You should just rub wild dandelions on behind your ears and then do some yoga!'

And there's always at least one prize knobber who leaves a comment saying, 'Did you know nine million people die PER MONTH from those killer superbugs that are living in hospital toilets! Oh yes, that's the truth!

My friend only went in to have her ingrown toenail examined and they carried her out four weeks later IN A WOODEN BOX!'

So Cava-Sue keeps sitting down beside my mother's bed, while my mother sleeps and then she cries a bit and then she gets angry, 'cos I won't read them and then I send her home to stop my father burning down any more of the kitchen trying to boil an egg and make toast. It's only now my mother's not there do we realise just how useless my dad really is at anything other than going to work and sitting on a chair reading the *Ilford Bugle*.

Anyway, I shouted at Cava-Sue today, 'No more printing out stuff off the internet! SAVE SOME PAPER YOU HYPOCRITE! I don't want to hear strangers' opinions on things.'

I called Uma today just to cheer myself up and she told me the same thing. 'Opinions are just like bumholes, Shiraz,' she said to me. 'Everyone's got one and they all stink. Just be there for your mum and take it day by day.'

'Innit, bruv,' I said but then I had to go 'cos I was standing in the hospital car park and I was freezing my bum off. It's proper annoying at the hospital when you want to make a phone call, 'cos you're not allowed to use your mobile inside the building. You've got to buy their special phone cards and use their special phones which cost about seven quid a minute, which would be quite reasonable if I was ringing Nigeria to ask how the Festival of Aragungu was going, but I'm only calling Goodmayes and that's three miles down the road.

So when I want to call someone, I have to go down to the front doors of the hospital and stand amongst all the chemotherapy people smoking fags wearing only their dressing gowns. Oh my dayz it is gross. They're puffing away on a Marlboro Red with the chemo drip actually attached to their arms.

It's such a bare disgusting thing to see that it's actually funny. Some of them are getting chemo for lung cancer. OH MY GOSH people are mentalists.

I was standing watching one of these geezers tonight, taking big thick drags of his Marlboro Red ciggie and blasting the fumes out of his mouth and nose into the air. He already looked about dead but he was obviously trying to finish himself off.

Just then I heard a voice beside me say, 'Ah good good everyone, keep puffing away, that's it. Good work!'

Well I turned around and it was Dr Okelloko, the doctor with the nice eyes.

'Hello,' I said, giggling a bit. I don't get to laugh much right now, but I like seeing Dr Okelloko 'cos he's always really calm and he's also got a wicked, quite sarcastic sense of humour. I suppose he has to really, 'cos he's surrounded by people dying all day long.

'How are you Shiraz Bailey Wood?' he said.

'Oh I'm all right,' I said. I was surprised he

remembered my name, 'I'm, well, y'know . . .'

'You're here every day aren't you?' he said. 'You must be tired.'

'Well, yeah,' I said. 'To be honest, I'd rather be here than at home right now. They're all panicking and getting on each other's nerves and . . . well at least when I'm here I can do some reading and stuff.'

'Yes I notice you're always reading,' he said. 'What are you reading at the moment?'

'Oh . . . I'm trying to re-read *Tess of the D'Urbervilles*,' I sighed. 'I've got exams coming up soon you see and—'

And then I stopped what I was saying.

What was I doing? I hadn't told anyone outside of school that. But there was something about talking to him that made me feel like I was in a different life completely. It was as if I was talking to someone who would understand, which was stupid as I didn't know Dr Okelloko at all.

'What are you studying for? Are you at university . . . Or are you doing A-levels?' he said, looking really interested.

'Oh, I'm just studying for mphgjghjh,' I mumbled. But then something happened that cut our conversation short anyway. 'Oh my days,' I said, 'That geezer with the chemo drip has just fallen out of his wheelchair. That's not good is it?'

'What?' said Dr Okelloko, spinning around, 'Oh God, I'd better pick him up. Not strictly my department but hey . . . anyway, see you later no doubt.'

'Thanks Dr Okelloko,' I said.

'Oh call me James, please,' he said. 'Well, only you are allowed to. I quite like the 'doctor' part usually. It makes me feel like a real doctor and not just someone going to a fancy dress party dressed as one.'

'OK, Dr James,' I said and then I wandered into the hospital leaving him wrestling a man in a tartan dressing-gown back into a wheelchair. I felt in a little bit of a better mood as I walked back to my mum's ward. Probably the happiest I'd been for about two weeks. Then I looked down at my hand and remembered that I'd forgotten to put that flipping ring of Wesley's on AGAIN, and instead of feeling happy I started to feel very guilty indeed.

TUESDAY 9TH MARCH

Murphy came up to the hospital with me tonight. Ritu was in London today and she hadn't come back when we left. She said she had a few things to sort out. I think she was maybe meant to be seeing the immigration people again and she's trying not to stress us any more.

Before she went I heard her nagging Murphy to get to the hospital and stop being a 'knobhead'. Sometimes I wish I'd never taught Ritu that word. She calls Murphy it a lot and I do feel a bit responsible. We both knew that.

Murphy has been trying to get out of any hospital visits. Ritu's quite upset with him, but I'm not so much 'cos I know why. I know that Murphy just can't handle seeing Mum not being strong, rock-hard Mum. He can't handle seeing her being this little, thin, weak thing breathing through a mask. He came with me last Friday night and you could see it broke his heart into millions of little bits. He sat there looking really upset then he disappeared and went and sat by the vending machines for half an hour with his head in his hands and his iPod on playing *Burial* which is this dub-step geezer who Murphy always listens to when he's got issues going on.

Most people don't treat my little brother like he's a boy any more, they treat him like a man 'cos he's six foot tall and he does weights twice a week with his mate Tariq so his shoulders are quite bulky. Murph sometimes even has a bit of a beard now and again when he can't be bothered to shave and when he's got face fur and and he wears his beanie hat pulled down and his coat buttoned right up well, yeah, he looks a bit psycho. But Murphy isn't a hard man at all. Not really anyway. He's nearly eighteen. He's sort of still a little boy but in a bloke's body. And I'm not slagging him for that. It's just the way things work out, innit?

When I see a lot of Murph's friends all acting like rudeboys and chatting about knives and guns and stuff I know deep down that they're still little boys and their brains haven't caught up with how their bodies look yet.

When Murph walked into the ward with me tonight my mother was lying out cold as she'd just had a load of painkillers and they'd made her woozy. Her mouth had fallen open, so I walked up and closed it for her, then got a tissue and wiped her eyes as they were all weeping. She didn't know we were there. I'm used to this now. That's why I always bring something to read with me 'cos she's away with the fairies most of the time. Murphy looked proper shocked.

'Mum?' he said, sitting down by her bed.

My mother never moved a muscle. She just let out a little grunt, a bit like a snore. He sat looking at her for a while and then he got up and touched her face with his hand, then he looked at me and his face was terrified. 'She's proper cold Shiraz! Ice cold. Is she breathing? Do the nurses come and look at her?' Murph stood up like he wanted to do something. 'How do we know she's OK? Shiraz what do we do?'

'Shush Murph,' I said, 'it's OK.'

And it's times like that when I just look at our Murph and it weirds me out 'cos his face is exactly the same as when he was a little lad. All those the times when we'd go shopping with Mother to ASDA and he'd be about four and I'd be six and Cava-Sue would be about eight. Well Cava-Sue would be all sensible and she'd just walk beside the trolley helping Mum find stuff. But me and Murph would be a nightmare, 'cos we'd run off and get lost completely and it would be funny for about the first ten minutes and then we'd realise we were completely lost. OUR MOTHER WAS GONE FOR GOOD.

Now for me this was the most exciting bit of all, 'cos if

we were really lucky we'd get found by the shop assistants and we'd get our names read out over the supermarket speakers and maybe even get taken to the office and get a biscuit and some squash to drink!

But Murphy didn't see the fun in this part at all. All he'd see was that Mother was gone and we'd never see her again EVER and his face would be pure TERROR and he'd want his mummy NOW! And his mouth would go all wobbly and his eyes all wide and watery and it was like it was the end of the world. He was always such a Mummy's Boy.

This was a bit like the face our Murph was pulling now, sitting by the hospital bed.

'Murph, chill out, bruv,' I said. 'She's OK. In fact this is probably the best she's looked for a long time.'

'Straight up?' he said.

'Tru dat, bruv,' I said. 'She's got a tiny bit of pink in her cheeks today. That's sort of amazing.'

'OK,' he said. Then he stood up and pushed a bit of hair away from her face again. Then he leaned over and kissed her cheek.

I know Murph and my mum have got a special bond. Him and her are as thick as thieves. She's always there with a spare tenner for him when he's skint, or with the time to quickly wash his favourite T-shirt when he wants it for a night out and she'll even answer his phone and tell people he's not in if he's avoiding someone. He'd be lost without her.

We both sat saying nothing for a while, staring at her sleeping for a bit, and then she started to move about a bit, like she was dreaming and then she opened her eyes and looked straight at us. Then she sort of tutted.

'Can I not get five minutes' peace?' she muttered. Then she sort of smiled at us and we both started giggling.

'Hello Mum,' said Murph. His face totally lit up. 'How do you feel?'

'Dog rough,' she said, 'like I've been run over by a horse. 'Ere Shiraz, was I run over by a horse at some point I don't remember?'

'Nah Mother,' I said. 'You weren't. I told you what's up with you. You've got something wrong with your lungs and erm, in your kidneys. They don't quite know yet.'

The thing I knew that none of the family did was that the doctors were checking her kidneys for cancer. But I hadn't let on anything about that, 'cos I knew everyone would lose the plot and they were bad enough already.

'Flipping doctors,' my mother muttered. 'There's one that comes in here faffing about. Brown skin, big brown eyes, Dr Cockaleekie or whatever he's called. Charming git, he thinks he is. Pghh! He's just a boy! He should be wearing short pants. I told him that too!'

'Oh good,' I sighed to myself, rolling my eyes. 'That'll keep everyone working hard to make you better.'

'How's the dog?' my mother said suddenly.

'Penny's fine. She's still fat,' I said. 'She's getting fed six times a day right now 'cos everyone keeps forgetting who has fed her last, so she's happy.'

I thought my mother was going to ask after us all then, but she didn't, she just shut her eyes again.

'Mum do you want us to bring you anything?' said Murph. Mum opened her eyes again then and looked at him.

'Where's Ritu?' she said. 'Those immigration lot haven't got her have they?'

'Erm, no, don't worry,' said Murphy, 'She's fine. She's just gone shopping today. It's all fine, Mum.'

'Is she still climbing up in that attic whenever anyone knocks on the door?' croaked Mum.

'Yeah,' said Murphy. 'But don't worry, Mum, it's gonna be fine. It's sorted.'

He seemed quite sure of that. I don't know why. Maybe he was just lying to make Mum feel better.

Poor Ritu, she's been spending half her life sitting in the attic surrounded by Cava-Sue's old A-level art projects and man they are all well emo. I don't know how long I'd manage to stay up there staring at the face of a crying clown made out of old eggshells in A3 size before I wished I was in the detention centre with the rest of the illegal foreigns.

My mother seemed quite tired again then. I put my hand on Murphy's shoulder and said, 'Come on, we should go and let her rest.' Just then my mother opened one eye and looked at me and said.

' 'Ere Shiraz, thank you sweetheart.'

'What for?' I said.

'For sorting everyone out,' she said. 'I know it's you keeping everything running.' Then she shut her eyes again and soon she was snoring.

Well I was gobsmacked when she said that. GOBSMACKED. I felt quite giddy as I walked back to the bus stop with our Murph thinking about what she said, but now I'm lying here in my bed I keep remembering what Mum said about 'keeping everything running' and about that interview at Manchester University in a few weeks' time and that letter from Oxford University that I've just been ignoring. I've started thinking Mum has a point. They do need me here in Essex. Not just Wesley, my whole family. There's no way I can leave them all and move away for good. Is there?

TUESDAY 16TH MARCH

Dear Baby Jesus Up Above,

How bad is it that H. Samuel the jewellers have called me twice in the last two days to say my engagement ring is now the correct size and is ready to collect, but I have been pretending to not get the calls? And if it is bad, can I be forgiven for it and also for the slightly rude dream I had about Dr Okelloko last night where I was dressed as a nurse and he was checking my reflexes which I am blaming on the Ice Cool Dorito sandwich I had before bed? It would be good if you could forgive me for all of this and quite soon, cheers blud – keep it real. SBW xxx

WEDNESDAY 17TH MARCH

OK, today felt like things were starting to turn a corner for the Wood family.

I went to the hospital after sixth form and when I got there my mother was actually sitting up in bed. Sitting up in bed being quite gobby to people which was a positive sign. Well not for the folk she was dissing but it was for me. There was a woman in the bed beside my mum complaining to her nurse that she couldn't hear her telly properly 'cos the volume was broken and my mother was saying to her, 'Well it's a wonder you can still hear anything at all with the noise you make when you're snoring, not to mention the other sounds coming out of OTHER PARTS OF YOUR BODY! Your ear drums must be shattered!'

Well the woman looked confused when my mother said that so my mother said, 'I meant your behind, love! Big trumps all night long! And I'm down wind of them!'

Well at this point I stepped in and told my mother to be quiet 'cos her painkillers were clearly making her say stuff she didn't mean, to which my mother just snorted and said, 'I mean every word I say!'

This did make me laugh 'cos it was amazing seeing her looking a bit feisty again.

Then she said, ' 'Ere, Shiraz, will you talk to those pillocks in the white coats and ask when I can go home. I'm sick of this hotel, I'd like to check out. One of them came and saw me before and said I'm getting better.'

'No they didn't,' I said. My mother is not a stranger to bending the truth to get her own way.

'He did,' she said. 'The boy with the big brown eyes, who's about eleven years old. He's probably gone off duty now, go and check the local Boys Scouts' hut.' I sighed at her when she said that. My mother will not be adding many names to her Christmas card list when she leaves this hospital. She's offended everyone from the receptionist to the Chief Surgeon.

'I'll have a word with them,' I said, 'but don't get your hopes up, you're still not well.'

The fact was she might have been looking a bit better but she was still nowhere near looking normal. She can't even put a straw into a carton of juice without having to have a long sleep afterwards to recover.

I wandered down the corridor and asked a few nurses if they had any info on my mother but none of them had. They all kept saying that I needed to wait for the doctor to do his rounds, so I said, 'When is that then?' and they all said, 'We've no idea,' and then went back to talking about *Home and Away* and warming their arses on the radiator on the wall.

Luckily, at that point I spotted Dr Okelloko or Dr Cockaleekie as my mother calls him walking through the double doors. I knew I was being cheeky, but I thought I'd grab him and ask if he could tell me anything as I was a bit confused.

'OK,' he said, giving me a wink. 'No problem.'

So we went into a little side office and he said that there was some new news about my mum. For the next ten minutes he said all sorts of big long words and pointed at a poster of a human body on the wall.

Basically, as far as I could understand, there are two separate things going on with my mum. One is her yucky lungs, but they were getting a bit better. The lung thing appeared to be caused by a chronic infection in her kidneys. And as far as they were beginning to see the kidney problem was responding to treatment. And as far as they'd done tests, there was nothing else to worry about in the kidneys. No cancerous lumps anyway. If everything went according to plan my mother in the long term could make a good recovery.

But this wasn't the end of the road, in fact she was still very ill indeed and she needed lots of rest and being looked after.

'But she's not going to die?!' I said.

'Well not that I can see at the moment. But I'd rather that you waited to hear all this from the senior specialist,' he said. 'But my guess is that she's going to be OK.'

I sat there with my mouth open for a second.

'Oh my God, I want to kiss you!' I said.

The doctor looked at me, then he raised one eyebrow. 'Well you can if you want,' he said. 'But I have a lot of patients to see, so please make it quick and, obviously, no tongues.'

Well I cracked up laughing when he said that, like it

was the funniest joke I'd ever heard.

'Thank you. Thanks for sorting her out. Thank you.'

'Well I'm glad we could help her. I can see you've all been exhausted with worrying about her,' he said. 'And you can maybe concentrate more on your studying now, eh?'

'Mmm, yeah,' I groaned. 'The final exams are getting really close. I've got a loads on.'

'What are you studying?' he said.

'Oh, er, A-levels,' I said. 'But it's like a secret. So could you please please not say anything to my mother, 'cos she'll probably have some sort of heart attack?'

He looked at me like he thought he was hearing things.

'You're doing secret A-levels?' he said.

'Yes,' I said.

'Secret ones?!' he repeated, looking at me like I was mental.

'Yes,' I nodded at him. 'No one knows. Apart from the sixth-form college and, erm, well you do now.'

He sat for a while and twiddled his pen and stared at me.

'But no one does secret A-levels,' he said. 'People secretly work as pole-dancers or hired assassins. But they don't sneak to school.'

'It's complicated,' I said.

'How complicated?' he said.

'You've met my mother haven't you?' I said.

James giggled a bit when I said that. 'Well yes, she is a very, er, spirited woman,' he said. 'And she does appear to have some very, er, strong views on life. She gives many

136

of the staff here a real, er, challenge.'

'You mean she's a nightmare don't you?' I laughed, 'cos I could see he was trying to use all professional words to make things smoother.

'Well, nightmare is an exceptionally strong word to use Miss Wood. In fact, I prefer, "challenging".' Then he looked at me and then pretended to examine his pen. Well this made me giggle. I liked his sense of humour 'cos it's a bit complex. He's a bit like me in the way he says cheeky things but sort of gets away with it 'cos of how he says them. And when I look at him I feel like there's a massive brain behind his eyes and he knows about tonnes and tonnes of stuff.

'Are you going to university?' he said.

'Mmm, dunno,' I said.

'Did you apply? Have you had any offers?' he said.

Well I couldn't lie to him. I had to tell someone the truth. 'Yeah, I got one from Manchester, to do English Literature. And one from Newcastle and one from . . . er . . . Oxford University.'

'Oxford? That's . . . brilliant!' he said. 'I went to Durham. I had friends who went to Newcastle and Manchester though. They're both good places. Do you have a first choice? Well, Oxford obviously!'

'Er . . . well, no . . . er,' I sort of mumbled. 'I still don't know what I'm doing.'

'What would stop you going, your family?' he said. 'Do you feel you need to look after your mother? You seem to have a big, strong family, Shiraz. Your sister is very capable and both of your brothers and your dad.'

I was going to point out I only had one brother but he was already carrying on talking about how people have to change and adapt to things and how he sees that all day long in the hospital and how I should just go for this as there's nothing like a few years at university. And forget about learning, there's also having fun. Meeting all kinds of people from all over the world, that sort of thing. But then his beeper began to squeak in his pocket, so he got interrupted. He picked up his pen again and swirled his email address and phone number on a piece of paper and gave it to me.

'If you want to know anything about Manchester, give me a shout and I'll put you in touch with my friend Horace. He studied architecture there,' he said. 'Oh and that's my number if you er, want to chat about anything else.'

'Cheers,' I said and folded up the paper and put it in my pocket. 'Oh my God, you should go! It's beeping again.'

'Yes I know,' he sighed. 'I know what it is though. I've got to go to ward nine and put a tube up an old man's bottom and then look through a camera at what is inside.'

'Oh my dayz,' I said. 'That is well disgusting.'

'Yeah,' he nodded. 'But it's my job. For ever. That's what I mean, go to university while you can and have some fun!'

I wandered out of the office and made my way back to my mum's bed feeling positive but really confused. Not only was I really psyched up about uni again, I appeared to have James's phone number in my pocket and an invite to call to chat about anything. Then I remembered the bit he said about 'both of my brothers' and realised that he thought Wes was my brother, not my boyfriend. I mean, why would he think any different? It's not like I kiss Wes much in public and I'm certainly not wearing the ring. And after that the piece of paper in my jeans pocket started to make me feel very guilty indeed.

The nurses say my mother should stay in hospital for at least another two weeks, unless she is very opinionated about it then they've no choice but to let her go home in a week. I'm hoping she'll be sensible and stay for two.

MONDAY 24TH MARCH

My mother discharged herself from hospital. I got a call on my mobile when I was at school from the hospital saying, 'Miss Wood, your mother has packed her things and called a mini-cab and signed herself out.'

'Oh my gosh,' I said. 'Is she well enough?'

The nurse sighed. 'Well she was walking like she had drunk seven pints, having to hold onto radiators to steady herself. We tried to make her sit in a wheelchair and be pushed by the porter but she wouldn't have any of it. And then she called one of the staff sisters "Bessie Balloonarse", and told her to go and get warm by the radiator, like she has been for the last month.'

'Oh dear,' I said, knowing exactly which nurse she meant. 'I am sorry. I think her painkillers are making her a bit . . .'

'Anyway she's gone,' said the nurse. 'Will someone be with her this afternoon?'

'Yeah,' I said, 'I'll go now.'

I ran to my locker at lunchtime. Asked Adu to get all my notes for this afternoon. Changed into my purple shirt and blue trousers and headed home. When I got to Thundersley Road my mother was sat on the sofa cuddled in with Penny, watching *Flog It* on BBC1. She was tiny and pale and weak but she was alive and that was the main thing.

'Hello Mother,' I said. 'Welcome home.'

She smiled at me, then nodded at her shelves of porcelain ladies that she's got by the telly.

'I see no one gave my Victorian nick-nacks a onceover with a duster while I was away,' she said. 'They're thick with dust.'

'I'll put the kettle on should I?' I said, smiling through slightly gritted teeth.

The woman is a pure nightmare, but it was amazing to have her home.

APRIL

SUNDAY 6TH APRIL

Looking after my mother is really hard work. She's a very bad patient, in fact at one point today I rang up the hospital and said I wanted to bring her back. She was refusing to take any of her medication, which is six little yellow pills and four white ones every twenty-four hours. I spent ages this morning stood beside her bed nagging her and at one point she started telling passers-by that I was trying to poison her.

'Are you, Shiraz? said Cava-Sue quite dryly. She'd come upstairs to see what all the noise was. 'Oh dear, that's not nice, is it? Why are you trying to poison Mummy? Why would anyone do that?'

'I'm not bloody poisoning her!' I huffed. 'I'm trying to get her to take the pills that she's meant to take.'

'I've had them pills already today,' Mother said. This was a lie.

'No, you haven't,' I said. 'You had those pills twenty-four hours ago. That was Saturday. Murphy gave them to you yesterday. You would take them yesterday for Murphy, wouldn't you? You took them good as gold!'

'Aw God bless our Murphy,' Mum said. Her eyes were lighting up, just remembering him. 'What a little soldier he is. He came in and said, "Mum I want you to take yer pills now," and then he counted them all out of the bottle himself!'

Mum looked genuinely touched just remembering this. 'Oh whoopie do! Call *Britain's Got Talent*,' I said. 'He's an eighteen-year-old boy. Not a King Charles spaniel! 'Course he can count pills out of a bottle.'

'And then he made sure I'd taken them all too! One by one!' my mother said.

I stood there silently fuming.

'Mother, just take the pills,' I said. 'Or else I'm taking the portable telly downstairs and you can forget watching the *EastEnders* omnibus.'

My mother narrowed her eyes at me. I thought I had her, but then she said calmly, 'I've had today's pills. It's you who isn't thinking straight.'

At this point I called the hospital and asked if I could bring my mother back as she was being difficult and a risk to herself, but unfortunately I got that nurse Mother called 'Bessy Balloonarse', and she just sniggered a bit and said that there were many things wrong with my mother and her kidneys were the least of it. She was meaning her personality! Then she put the phone down laughing! Oh my dayz! How rude!

I would have tried to sue the NHS for some compo money for my damaged feelings but the fact was that the nurse was totally right. It's like looking after a cross between a four-year-old and an angry

Tyrannosaurus Rex most days. Anyway, eventually I got my mother to swallow her medication for me, then me and her got along a lot better.

Those pills certainly are making her stronger 'cos once she'd had a little nap she spent the whole afternoon nagging Cava-Sue about getting Fin's hair cut into a short back and sides 'cos if she doesn't he will 'end up being one of them gays'.

My mother is obsessed with Fin turning out to be gay. She's trying to ban Maisy the Mouse 'cos it is encouraging Fin to like having imaginary tea parties (which is 'gay', apparently) and she's encouraging Fin to play with an old fake plastic machine gun that used to belong to Murphy. Oh and she's hidden his pink wellies with the ducks on them. (Also 'gay'.)

'Mother,' Cava-Sue was saying today. 'Plenty of little boys like Maisy Mouse. And I let Fin choose those wellies. he likes them! He likes ducks!'

'Yes, well,' mum said. 'All I'm saying is there's nothing wrong with a nice toy gun! That's what little boys like. All Murphy's crowd used to play with guns!'

'Mother, most of Murphy's old crowd are now in Feltham Young Offenders'!' Cava-Sue shouted. 'They never quite stopped playing with guns did they? Two of them shot Mr Patel who runs the Post Office in the shoulder for forty quid and a box of Curly Wurlies!'

'Oh, stop being dramatic,' my mother said. 'I suppose you'd rather your Fin was stood on the back of some lorry wearing a woman's dress in twenty years' time would you!? On that Gay Pride march thing they all do!?'

'Actually Mother, yes I would!' said Cava-Sue, 'I don't care what Fin does with his life as long as he's happy and safe. He's my son and I love him!'

Well, then my mother pointed out that Fin even talks like a girl which made Cava-Sue even more het up and she started going on about 'sexist stereotypes', and the row went on for ever which was actually really useful 'cos it gave me a nice long afternoon to study some History. As I listened to my mum and Cava-Sue squabbling, I could hear that although they were both cross, at some level they were both enjoying themselves 'cos they both kept laughing, and at one point Cava-Sue stopped midway through her ranting and said, 'Ooh I'm parched, do you fancy a cup of tea and a chocolate mini-roll?' And my mum said, 'Ooh lovely. 'Ere, there's a bit of madeira loaf in the tin too! Spread some jam on a bit for me and bring it up.' And when I went in later they were both in bed watching the *EastEnders* omnibus.

It was just like old times.

WEDNESDAY 9TH APRIL

Mum asked me today if I had heard anything from GMTV about that 'win a wedding' competition thing and I said, 'Ooh no, not a word. I think they must have forgotten about it.'

'No Shiraz, Darleen was talking about it the other day!' Mum said. 'They're going to make an announcement this month! Four couples are going to go down to three!'

'Well, I've not heard anything,' I said.

'Well, have they not rung your Wesley?' she said, eating the toast with Marmite that I'd just made her.

'No, I don't think so.' I said. 'Wesley's sort of busy though, Mother. He's working flat out on those new Tanorife shops ain't he?'

'Well, will you ring him and see if he's had any messages?' Mum said. ' 'Cos you two could be wed by the end of the year if this competition comes off, couldn't you?'

'Yeah,' I said.

'I reckon you've got a good chance of getting this,' she said. 'It was a masterpiece that form I sent in!'

'Hmmm, I bet,' I said, taking her plate away.

' 'Ere,' mum said, wiping crumbs off her dressing gown. 'When they ring you, just say yes to everything right? 'Cos some of it might sound a bit odd. Y'know, your life-history and stuff.'

'What do you mean?' I said.

'Oh, that bit on the form where you've got to say why you think you deserve to win. Any stories, that kind of thing.'

'Aw Mother,' I tutted. 'You didn't tell them about the time I worked as the elf at the House of Hardy Christmas grotto did you? Or the time Wesley was part of the G-Mayes Detonators rap syndicate? You haven't told them that Wes used to do human beatbox or anything have you?'

'Human beatwhat?' she said. 'Is that something mucky?'

'Noooo it isn't!' I said.

'Well, no. I've not said anything about that anyway. I've just . . .' she started, but then she stopped. 'They've not called you though? You're sure?'

'Yes, I'm sure!' I said, taking her plate downstairs and washing it and then sneaking off to school. I mean, yeah, I've had a few missed calls and one message from a woman called Isabella who wanted me to call her back 'ASAP' but I'm sure that was nothing to do with that and I've deleted it now anyway.

THURSDAY 17TH APRIL

Today was a bit of a disaster. I feel so stupid. Why have I let myself get carried away with this idea of going to university? It's not for people like me at all. I know Ms Bracket is a proper nice lady and she's trying to help me and I'm sure it would be well satisfying for her to get someone as common as me into a place like Manchester University, but I don't think she's keeping it real at all. Not after what happened today anyhow.

Basically, I got up this morning and I knew I had to go

to Manchester for my Open Day. I was feeling terrible about it so in the end I decided to call Carrie. I wondered if she'd be around to come along, even though I'd need to come clean about all the lies I was telling. Plus I'd need to swear her to secrecy, which would be hard 'cos she's got a gob like the Eurotunnel.

I just really needed some support. Cazza is really good at supporting 'cos when she goes to something scary like that she's so on a different planet and says such random stuff that's it's easy to forget what you're scared about. When me and Carrie are together I feel double powerful, that's why she gets me into trouble a lot. So I called her up but when she picked up her phone she sounded in a weird mood.

'Aight, what's happening?' I said.

'I'm at work,' she said, sadly.

'You're where?!' I said.

I tried to think of lots of other words that rhymed with work that she could have meant. Berk? Lurk? Perk? Merk? Carrie couldn't have said 'work'. Carrie ain't got a job. Carrie's spent the last six months telling her father she's applying for jobs but then forgetting to post the letters, or forgetting to enclose a CV, or forgetting to send a covering letter with the CV and even when she remembers all of it at once, she never gets any answers 'cos of her C.V. She's got a criminal record, plus on her hobbies section it just says, 'pizza and chillaxing'.

'I'm at work,' she said again, 'At Tanorife.'

'Oh my God, when did that happen?!' I said.

'Pghghhghgh,' she sighed. 'Well you can thank your fiance Wesley Barrington Bains II actually, Shiraz. He met my father in the plumbers' supplier stores on Saturday. And he only starts telling him that Collette is looking for girls to work in the new shops, doesn't he? And piff paff bloody poooff, look at me. I'm here. I'm in Romford!'

'Oh my dayz,' I said. 'But that store ain't even open is it yet?'

'Not for two weeks! Wes is still fitting all of the bathrooms. One of the shower rooms is still a broom cupboard at the moment,' said Carrie. 'I'm just sitting here with Carly Carrington stuffing envelopes with vouchers and doing a mail-out to all the clients. Hey do you remember Carly? She was at my party?'

'Carly Carrington is there too?' I said.

'Yeah,' said Carrie. 'Oh she is funny. Me and her have been having a giggle actually. And Wes is around too, so it's not been so bad for the last few days. But it's still hard work. I have to work until 3.30pm! That is seven and a half hours I'm working today!'

I was trying to sound sympathetic but I was feeling a bit weird about Carly Carrington and Wes working together all day long. I hope she knows he's engaged now. ENGAGED. I hope Carrie has told her.

'Shizzle,' Carrie said. 'This has well mucked up my plans to watch *The OC* right from Season One. It was starting today on T4. I'm devastated bruv.'

I just laughed when she said that.

'And that pig of a father of mine says that if I don't stick it here for at least a year he's cutting off my allowance,' she said. 'Can you believe it? And he's still quacking on about that New Year's Eve party saying the bannister is damaged like people have been sliding down it. I think he's having a mid-life crisis or something! Well I told him if he's sick of me he should cough up the cash so me and Bezzie can get our own flat. But he won't!'

'He is sooo unreasonable,' I said, trying to sound genuine. Carrie is a brat. I love her, but she is a brat. One hundred percent. No arguments.

'Anyway, what can I do for you?' she said. 'Do you want a tan or something? I can do you mates' rates.'

'Oh no,' I said. 'I was just going to ask you if . . . actually Cazza it don't matter. It don't matter at all. I'll ring you tomorrow. You still want to go down Vue and watch that Lindsay Lohan thing?'

'Yeah,' she said. 'If I haven't died of slave labour by then.'

'Well, you stay strong eh?' I said and put the phone down.

I was going to have to do this Manchester thing alone.

I caught the commuter train from Goodmayes to Liverpool Street and then the tube to Euston station in London, where I bought a Virgin train ticket to Manchester Piccadilly. The 11am train was packed.

151

Almost every single seat was pre-booked which meant I ended up sitting facing backwards next to this enormous woman in a double seat who was hogging far more than double of it. Now travelling backwards makes me confused at the best of times, but it wasn't being made any better by this woman, who for the whole journey kept rummaging between her thighs and picking stuff out of a Marks and Spencer Simply Food bag that she had on the floor, then pushing them into her face. So by the time we'd reached a place called Rugby she'd demolished a Duck in Hoi Sin Sauce wrap, twelve Californian sushi rolls, a Banoffi Pie, a five-hundred-gram bag of Cheesy Puffs, two bottles of Dandelion and Burdock and a bag of cola bottles. By this point I was proper intrigued to see what she was going to eat next. I was also dying to go for a wee but I was trying to keep it in, 'cos I'm scared of those train toilets with the big automatic door that opens and closes. 'Cos it says when you're inside that if you press the red button and the light comes on then it's locked but I don't believe this ever since me and Cazza went to see Black Eyed Peas at Milton Keynes Bowl and we were on the train there and I thought I'd locked it but I HADN'T and the door swung open and the whole carriage saw me sitting doing a widdle with my jeans and thong down by my ankles, playing snake on my mobile phone! IT WAS ONE OF THE WORST MOMENTS OF MY LIFE.

So anyway, the journey to Manchester today was

horrible, what with amazing eating woman and my bladder and the fact I had some bloke sat across from me playing death metal on his iPod the whole way there. Eventually, I arrived at Manchester and the train doors opened and I thought, 'OH MY GOD IT IS FREEZING!' 'cos it felt like it was about minus five and it was raining too and it was that sort of rain that goes sideways and soaks you no matter what. HOW CAN IT BE SO COLD IN MANCHESTER? It's only about six centimetres away on the map? This is the furthest North I have ever been in my life and it was a proper shock to my system. No wonder everyone in *Coronation Street* is always either drunk or in bed with each other or in the house eating fishfingers and huddled around a gas fire. It's to keep warm. It was at this point that I wished I'd put on a scarf and Cava-Sue's llama-skin hat and some snowboots instead of my stupid pink hoodie and jeans and slip-on ballet shoe things from Top Shop, which were no use whatsoever. So I walked through the train station staring at all the people walking around in no coats and just T-shirts. Or girls with mini-skirts on with no tights or anything, just pale blue bare legs. In fact I wanted to walk up to them and go, 'Are you mental or something? You're going to die of cold!' but then I realised they must be used to it. Like maybe they've got thicker blood.

So then I went to find the bus to the university, and when I'm standing at the bus-stop this woman suddenly says to me, 'Ooh, isn't it parky today Chuck, eh?' So I looked at her funny and I thought, 'Do I know you?' And then she said, 'Aye, I've just got us back from two weeks in Spain. Ooh it were right smashing, grand-kiddies fair enjoyed it. Pools n'at. Slides. Magic.'

Well it took me a while to be able to translate this weird language she was speaking in, but I could pick up enough words to know that she was chatting about the weather and her holidays. Oh and that she didn't know who I was at all. She was just chatting to me 'cos I was stood there.

That's what people always say about people up North, don't they? They even chat to each other if they don't know each other! Well I thought I'd show willing so I said, 'I've never been to Spain but I've been to Ibiza.'

Well, that was it then, she never shut up for about half an hour. I got her whole life story, including the fact she's just been in hospital and had three metres of her stomach removed and then she started pulling her coat up to show me the scar! In fact I only managed to get off the bus at the right stop by pinging the bell ten times and hurdling over the tartan shopping trolley, 'cos she wouldn't let me out.

'Ta-ra petal!' she shouted as I went.

So then I found the University building where the English department was. Outside there was quite a lot of studenty types stood holding folders, chatting and smoking, plus lots of kids standing with their mums and dads who looked all lost, so they had to be on the Open Day too. I felt quite nervous then, 'cos no one looked at all like me. The girls all looked like those sensitive types of girls who wear cardigans and eat *cous cous* and listen to Dido albums and went to posh all-girls schools and have probably already taken a year out to build an Aids orphanage and teach lepers in Brazil how to do the 'Crank That Soldier' dance. And all their mums and dads looked proper clever and serious and looked like they were teachers or accountants. They were telling their kids what questions to ask inside and inquiring whether the fees would be paid monthly or term-by-term and whether they could do it by electronic bank transfer and whether it would help if they went in and spoke to a tutor on their behalf. I felt really alone. So then I walked inside the building and there was a girl in a pink tutu and a bright green cardigan with dyed red hair sitting on a chair near the office reading a hand-out about the English course and she was moaning really loudly.

'Oh God, I've read most of these books already? Do we really have to do a whole term devoted to *fin de siecle* British Literature? Can I skip that and take a unit in like, Japanese or something a bit more challenging?' Then she looked at me and said, 'It's hardly inspiring is it? I mean who hasn't read Robert Louis Stephenson and HG Wells? I think my nanny read me those ones!'

Well, I felt like crying then. Before Ms Bracket came to Mayflower Academy one of the only books I'd ever finished was *Forever* by Judy Blume and that was only 'cos it had mucky bits in it about boys' thingies.

This day was turning out to be a big mistake.

Why do I think I can actually study English Literature at uni? I tagged on to a little group who were off the uni tour, but by now I was cold, I was hungry, I still needed a wee and I was feeling like a simpleton.

For the next few hours I wandered with a group of posh girls in cardigans looking at stuff like the library (which looked exactly like a library), and the university halls of residence (which reminded me of the time me and Carrie went to visit Knighty in Feltham Young Offenders Institute). And then I saw inside one of the flats which smelled a bit of wee and toast. The bedrooms were about three metres by three metres and yellow/grey coloured and had old BluTack all over the walls and the same curtains that are in the nurse's sick-bay area at school. Oh, and a bathroom that I would be sharing with about ten other people with a shower that was full of pubes.

By this point I'd made up my mind. I was going home and never coming back.

'What do you think?' said one girl in a velour head band who was wearing a 'Save the Gnu' T-shirt and some brown cords and baseball boots that she's personalised herself by drawing squirrels on with a felt tip.

'Mmmm,' I said, trying not to start sobbing there and then. 'It's a bit basic.'

'Yah, I know,' she said, but she sounded proper cheery. 'My big sister says not to worry though, 'cos apparently when you get all your things in, it feels really cosy. And after a few weeks you can't imagine the room not being yours. And it's meant to be a real giggle living here. People have parties all the time! Oh and the uni has an AMAZING juggling society! Do you juggle?'

'Pardon?' I said.

'Do you juggle?' she said.

'Juggle what?' I said.

'Oh, you know,' she said. 'Balls, hoops, bananas! That sort of thing!'

'No,' I said. 'I don't know how to.'

'Oh, you should learn! It's so relaxing! It really frees your mind! I learned to juggle in Tibet while I was on my gap year working in a monastery feeding the street children!'

About an hour after that I was on the train home. I've sat in my bedroom ever since staring at the ceiling thinking about everything that happened today. And thinking what is the point in passing these A-levels if that's what uni is like? And if I did go, there's no way Wes will come with me 'cos he'd feel like even more of a spare part than I would.

I felt so confused in the end that I went and got some fruit from the kitchen and had a go at juggling. But it didn't free my mind whatsoever. 'Cos if you don't know how to do it then you're basically just chucking apples about and smashing them on the floor and that's not a circus skill at all is it?

Not even at a really rubbish circus.

THURSDAY 24TH APRIL

Damn. I picked up my phone on the way home from Lidl tonight without checking who was calling and it was that Isabella woman. Isabella from *GMTV*. She was wondering if I could do a live phone-call on the show tomorrow at 7.30am. Just to discuss the exciting news that me and my fiance Wesley are now in the FINAL three to win the dream wedding.

'Oh er,' I said. 'Well, I'm sort of working then I think I'll have to . . .'

'Oh, at Lidl? You work full-time there don't you?' she said. 'Well we can call you there! It will only take five minutes. I'm sure the manager won't mind. Do you want me to phone him?'

'NO!' I said. 'Don't ring Lidl. Actually I've just realised, I'll be at home.'

'Oh, good,' she said. 'So you can do it?'

'Yeah, er, I suppose so,' I said feeling really in a corner now. 'What do you want me to talk about?'

'Oh, it's just a general chat about why you really really would love to win the wedding,' she said. 'Just to give our audiences a good idea why they should text in and vote for you. I mean, considering your story, I'm sure they will anyhow. No one deserves it like you do, really.'

'Do you think?' I said. 'We've only been engaged a couple of months. I'm sure the other girls are more deserving of it than me. One of the girls only has one foot hasn't she? Hasn't she been saving up for years for special bridal shoes?'

'Mmmm, yes Shiraz,' said Isabella. 'But I do think your story will capture the public's imagination. It's quite spectacular. And you don't mind discussing everything do you? I mean, Darleen will be tactful to sensitive matters obviously.'

'Er . . . OK,' I sighed, 'cos she was starting to hack me off a bit really with all this mushy language. Sensitive matters? I'm not discussing any sensitive matters on telly! She can jog on, bruv, big time.

'Look Darleen can ask me whatever she wants,' I said, as politely as I could. 'If I don't want to answer I don't have to. Is that fair?'

'Yes of course,' she said. We'll call you tomorrow at 7.20am so can you please be by your phone.'

'OK,' I said to her. And then she put the phone down. I suppose the one good thing about tomorrow is that it is my chance to kill this whole wedding competition for good. Don't you worry missing-foot-woman, I'm going to get you those shoes if it kills me.

FRIDAY 25TH APRIL

Y'know, I thought I'd run out of ways to be surprised by the behaviour of my family, but no. Oh no, no no no no! Each day there are new types of shame on offer. OH MY DAYZ, I am really really flipping angry at the moment. LIVID in fact. And yes I know I should be trying to do the counting thing and the breathing thing but I want to get this all down in my diary instead, so I can remember it in full detail for whenever I feel guilty about leaving this bunch of blithering HEADCASES and changing my phone number and never calling them again ever.

Y'know, I have been reading in the newspaper recently about more and more children actually divorcing their families for being annoying and I was thinking, 'That's a bit tight,' but on further thought I think that's a pretty good idea. In fact when I've calmed down I'm going to the Town Hall to get the necessary paperwork!

OK – BREATHE SHIRAZ BREATHE – so I get up at 6.30 this morning and have a cup of coffee and then have another one 'cos I need to be fully awake for when this woman rings. Cava-Sue was downstairs too and she'd bribed Fin with his breakfast to be quiet and my mum and Murphy and Ritu are all there in their pyjamas gathered around the portable telly in the kitchen waiting for the call. They have to watch in the kitchen because I'm not allowed to have the sound up on the telly in the living room while I talk to Darleen because it will cause all sorts of funny noises and feedback, which would 'sound horrible', although not as horrible as the parrot which *GMTV* have had in the studio for the last hour who can play the theme tune from *The Bill* on a xylophone. Adults put this kind of crap on breakfast telly and then wonder why young people always stay in bed until 2pm.

So at about 7.20am the phone rang and it was a researcher from *GMTV* saying they were about to put me through. So I took a deep breath and my stomach felt all squelchy, but I thought:

'Right you can do this Shizzlebizzle. It's going to be fine. Just keep it real.' Then before I knew it I was on the phone LIVE ON AIR to Darleen and she was asking me all about how excited I must be to be marrying the man of my dreams and exactly how I would feel if I got to wear the sixteen-thousand pound designer gown which had a long 'train' of material on the back which was four metres of finest antique *Broderie Anglaise* lace! And how would I feel to cut the seven-tier cake which was made by the same chefs who make royal wedding cakes!?

'Er, yeah it will be good,' I said. 'Like, er . . . a dream come true.'

My mother stuck her head round the living-room door at this point and mouthed the words, 'Liven it up you miserable git!' at me. I scowled back at her.

'I can't wait!' I said. 'It's what I've been dreaming about since I was a little girl!'

Well when I said that, Darleen put her head to one side like she was about to cry and she said:

'Oh, and I suppose that's what kept you going when you were a little girl wasn't it? Through all those terrible times?'

'Um, how do you mean?' I said. Alarm bells started to go off in my head then. I should have just hung up but I wanted to know what she meant.

'Well, I know you won't mind me telling the viewers about this, but yours was a very tragic childhood wasn't it?' she said, really sadly.

'Er, well,' I said.

'I'm sure you had lots of time to imagine your dream wedding when you were locked in the garden shed.'

'The shed?' I said.

'Yes, when you were a little girl, before you were adopted by the Wood family,' she said. 'You were adopted at the age of twelve after a very traumatic childhood, weren't you? You were fed on dog biscuits until you were aged eight and kept in a garden with Jack Russell terriers weren't you? In fact when your adoptive mum Diane first met you, you could only communicate in barks and howls. It's such a heartbreaking story.'

I sat for a bit, absolutely gobsmacked. This was total rubbish. I am not adopted. I've lived in Thundersley Road all my life! There's photos everywhere to prove it. My mother has been telling some massive WHOPPING fibs on this form. She's been stealing

162

storylines from those miserable books she reads and mixing them all up and passing them off as mine! That woman is a flaming liability!

I didn't know what to do, so I said in a very sarcastic voice:

'I know, Darleen, it is unbelievable isn't it, I don't know how I coped but I did.' My mother appeared at the door again then and she was giving me two thumbs-up signs and smiling!

'Well, you must have remarkable inner strength,' Darleen said. 'Is it true that you can catch a ball from ten metres away in your mouth?'

I couldn't believe what I was hearing. At this point I heard Murphy almost wetting his underpants with laughter and say, 'Oh Mother, I can't believe you left that bit in. I only added that for a laugh!'

MURPHY WAS IN ON THIS TOO!

'Darleen,' I said, my face had started to go the colour of one of my nan's jars of pickled beetroots by now, 'I'm finding this very difficult to discuss.'

'Oh, we understand,' she said. 'We need to go to the news now, but thank you so much for joining us. Goodbye! And that was Shiraz Bailey Wood everyone, who is one of the most deserving dream brides I think this competition has ever seen. Please send in your texts if you agree!'

I threw the phone down and went through to the kitchen where they were all sitting. Cava-Sue was standing there holding Fin, her gob was wide open and she was totally speechless. My mother was suddenly pretending to be ill again.

'Ooh, I think I might need a lie down, my kidneys are giving me jip,' she said. 'I'll have this tea in bed.'

Meanwhile Murphy was almost dying from laughing. 'HAHAHAHAHAHAHHAHAHAHHA!' he roared, until Ritu punched him on the arm and he shut up.

'Murphy, this is NOT funny!' I shouted. 'The whole nation now thinks I was raised by dogs and lived in a shed until I was twelve! Do you think this is funny!?'

Well Murphy obviously did as he was laughing again now so hard I thought we were going to have to fetch him clean trousers.

'Oh, Shiraz, stop being so dramatic,' said my mother. 'Look, OK, fair play, I'll put me hands up, I may have bended the truth a touch but I was only doing the best for my little girl! What mother wouldn't? I wanted your application to stand out.'

This might have softened me up a bit if I didn't know how excited she was about the eight-hundred-quid Marks and Spencer 'Mother of the Bride' voucher which was part of the deal.

'Well, it's certainly done that, Mother! Me and Wes are in the final three! Mother, this whole thing is a pack of lies and you know it!'

'Phghghgh,' spluttered my mother. 'Oh everyone lies in these things. I mean that girl with the missing foot?

164

How do we know she's not faking that?'

'HOW CAN YOU FAKE A MISSING FOOT?!' I shouted. And I was shouting now, really shouting. And my fists were scrunched too.

'Oh, of course you can fake a missing foot,' my mother was saying while buttering more toast. 'I watched that David Blaine the magician on telly the other night. He made the Empire State Building disappear. IT DON'T MEAN HE DID IT.'

'Oh, I've had enough of you lot,' I fumed. 'You've crossed a line this time.'

'Shiraz!' cried Murphy. 'Shiraz, calm down, calm down . . . hey do you want me to get you a bowl of water or anything? HA HA HA HA HA HA!'

Well, I was so livid then that I stormed out of the kitchen, slamming all of the doors and have been sat here in my bedroom ever since. I've got nothing more to say to any of them. NOTHING.

MAY

TUESDAY 6TH MAY

When I came out of the underground station at Sloane Square in London today I felt a bit shaky, 'cos I don't know that area of the city very well at all.

Chelsea is really intimidating. It's full of posh people carrying piles of posh boutique bags and Mercedes Benzes and Range Rovers whizzing past and whole classes of little rich children trotting along in straw hats and tweed uniforms and nannies pushing double buggies and catwalk models in dark glasses rushing to model castings. It's like London would look if you were watching it in a Lindsay Lohan movie. How London is supposed to look. Not at all like where me and Cazza used to live in East London in Whitechapel which was well scuzzy really, and you used to find rats eating your rubbish and the only cars down our street were stolen ones clamped with the windows smashed.

In Chelsea the streets are clean and full of ancient houses that are about five floors high and the fronts are painted pure white and the spiked railings outside are pure white too and the front doors are glossy and black with silver polished doorknobs.

I walked for about twenty minutes when I got out of

the tube station, checking the GPS map on my mobile phone, getting proper confused. I wasn't sure which way I was meant to be holding the map up. I needed to find King James Mews, which was just off Ballington Avenue London SW1. Eventually, I made a few correct turns and it all started to come together.

I wish I had more faith in myself when it comes to maps. I always let my Wesley do it usually 'cos he says map-reading isn't a girl's thing. Wesley says girls and maps are a liability and that's why girls shouldn't be in the army or even ambulance drivers 'cos they'd end up driving their tanks or ambulances the wrong way completely. Wesley says it's OK if women need to drive to get to the beautician's and take their kids to school but not when it's a life and death scenario.

He's not even kidding when he says this either. I tell him that he's being sexist but Wes says to me that I always say stuff is sexist 'cos I want to be politically correct all the time and it's not like that in the real world. Wes says the truth is that women are rubbish at some things and good at others and that's why he's rubbish at tidying and stuff 'cos it's really a girly thing.

When me and Wes first got together he used to say stuff like this in a jokey way to wind me up but nowadays I know that deep down he really means it and that's why he leaves his boxer shorts in a little pile on the floor beside the washing basket every day and never puts them in.

I turned off Ballington Avenue and into this little cobbled sidestreet and walked along looking for Number 8. Soon it was in front of me, a dark blue door with four doorbells for the different flats. Beside the third bell down was the letter C and a little name tag that said 'Brunton-Fletcher/Bryson'. I stared at it for a moment, feeling a bit scared, then put my finger on the bell and pressed it. A voice came through the little speaker beside the bell and shouted, 'Hello?!'

'Erm . . . hello!' I said, 'It's Shiraz Bailey Wood here. Is that you Uma?' There was a little pause. I thought I'd got the wrong flat.

'No, it's Aaliyah!' said the voice. She sounded friendly though. Thank God!

Sometimes I get scared when I meet new people. I don't know why, I just do.

'Uma is here though, Shiraz! Hang on, I'm buzzing you in!'

Then there was a loud HRRRRRRRRRNK and I was in the lobby which was painted pure white with a pink welcome mat and a massive yucca plant on table.

This place was really nice. Proper posh. I was so pleased for Uma. I remember the times when she lived with her family and everything was always so crazy that sometimes she didn't have a bed. She had to sleep on the floor with no mattress. Y'know sometimes I could hate Rose for what she did to Uma, but now I think it's just a proper waste of an emotion 'cos the silly cow doesn't know any better, 'cos Rose's own mother was even worse. This is why Uma is so amazing. She worked hard and she's broken the pattern of crap following more crap. Uma is amazing really, I'm glad that people have started to see that.

I walked up the staircase and as I got up to the first floor I could hear a voice above me saying, 'Shiraz Bailey Wood? Well I can't say this is a surprise. I've been expecting you at some point.'

I started laughing when I heard that. It was Uma. As I turned the corner she was stood there looking really pretty but rock hard as ever in black close-fitting track pants and a black vest top. All her hair was gathered up on her head in a band, she had a pair of diamond earrings on and there was a nicorette patch stuck on her arm.

'Aight Uma!' I said.

'Shizzlebizzle!' she said, and she gave me a big hug. Then Zeus came running out and put both paws up on my shoulders and licked half my foundation off with three big licks of his enormous slobbering tongue.

'Look Zeus!' said Uma, 'it's Aunty Shiraz! I said she'd come to London, didn't I?'

'How did you know?' I said.

'Well you were bound to weren't you? I reckoned you'd need a wedding-dress fitting,' Uma said. 'Or y'know . . . to come through and find a wedding cake. . . . or y'know, to run away from everything and need somewhere to hide.'

I started to blush now.

'Hmmm,' I said. 'Is the kettle on?'

'I'll put it on,' she said. 'And then do you want to tell me what's really going on?'

So I walked into the flat and I met Uma's friend Aaliyah who is really really lovely and funny. She's small with short blonde hair and big green eyes, but I wouldn't want to get on the wrong side of her, 'cos she does kickboxing and she's basically all muscle with no body fat at all. Uma and Aaliyah both had two days off from where they work at Mr Deng's new casino in Chelsea Harbour called 'Fortune Fountain', that's where all the really 'high rollers' gamble. These are the folk that can afford to lose millions of pounds in one night!

'That's how Mr Deng has the cash for his staff to live in places like this,' said Aaliyah, who was chopping up vegetables and putting them into a posh, dark red casserole dish. 'You never see a skint casino boss do you? There's punters in that casino all day every day losing money as fast as they can!'

'Yep,' agreed Uma. 'Y'know that's probably the only useful thing I ever learned from my so-called father in Portsmouth. He gambled away every penny he ever had on the dogs or betting on football or on horses. I used to look at him when I was younger and think all that money of his must be going somewhere! I want to work wherever that's going!'

I sat and drank my tea and ate some chocolate

brownies that Aaliyah has just made that morning. It felt AMAZING to be away from Essex and my mother and from faking being at Lidl and the daily updates on Tanorife from Wes and from Carrie or Murph and Ritu worrying about immigration. Actually, now I thought about it, Murph and Ritu didn't seem to be too bothered about that any more. It was like they'd started living in an amazing deep sense of denial about life, like I had.

'So, Shizzle,' said Uma. 'Are you going to tell me what's going on?'

'Oh, nothing,' I said. It was the least convincing 'nothing' in the world ever.

'Well have you come through to ask me officially to be bridesmaid?' smiled Uma. ''Cos Carrie and Kez say I'm one and, y'know, it would be good to put a date in the diary, 'cos I don't wanna double book and have to turn up in my casino uniform. Bruv, this is the one chance in your whole life to see me in a pretty dress. You better get some photos of this!'

'Mmmm,' I said. Then Uma sat staring at me for ages, doing that thing she does where she shuts up and it makes you talk just to fill the silence. Uma has learned this from the cops always being at her house when she was tiny. Apparently it's a thing the CID do.

'Unless there's something I don't know about?' Uma said eventually. 'Ooh, a bit like the Plan B you were talking about at New Year's Eve.'

I took a deep breath. Uma was glaring right at me.

Aaliyah was stirring something in a pan, pretending to be listening to the radio.

'OK,' I said. 'OK I've got to tell you everything. EVERYTHING!'

'HALLELUJAH!' said Uma.

'I'm living a lie!' I said. 'One big massive ginormous LIE!'

'OK . . . ha ha ha, oh this is good!' laughed Uma. 'Keep going!'

'I don't work full-time at Lidl!' I said to her. 'I'm sitting my final A-level exams in about three weeks' time.'

I felt pounds lighter already. Uma was really laughing. 'And I've had some offers from universities! From Manchester and Newcastle! To begin in October!'

'Aaliyah, can I have a ciggie? This is a special occasion!' said Uma.

'Aw babe, said Aaliyah, 'but you've done so well. Have some more chewing gum instead!'

'What else?!' said Uma, poking me in the arm.

'And I've said yes to marrying Wes. And I DON'T really want to get married. I don't mean never ever. I mean maybe in ten years' time. But not now,' I said. 'Wes doesn't know anything about the A-levels. In fact no-one does really.'

'Unbelievable,' said Uma, chomping away on her gum furiously.

'But then I went for this Open Day at Manchester Uni,' I said. 'And it was awful! And now I don't think

Uni is the place for me either! 'Cos it ain't is it? The people there would never just accept me for who I am if I'm being me. Y'know, keeping it real and all that? Would they?'

Uma just looked at me and rolled her eyes.

'Oh shut up, you donut,' she said. 'Of course they would. You're a complete legend, Shiraz Bailey Wood. Of course you could go to Manchester University. You'd walk it. You were made for uni, Shiz!'

'Mmmm,' I said. 'But there's another thing.' Then I opened my handbag and got out the letter I've been carrying about for months. I passed to it to Uma and she took it out of the white crumpled envelope which was covered in finger marks and coffee stains and she read it.

'OH MY DAYZ!' she said.

'I know,' I said.

'What is it?' said Aaliyah.

'It's from Oxford University,' Uma said. 'Shiraz has been offered a conditional place. It's an invite to go up and visit them.'

'Wow!' said Aaliyah. 'That's amazing! When are you going?'

I sat there and stared back at them. Then I examined my nail varnish. They were both still staring at me.

'You're going, Shiraz,' said Uma. 'I ain't taking any backchat about this. You're going. And that's that. No arguments.'

I suppose that's the good thing about Uma Brunton-

Fletcher. She makes things that seem really really complicated, really really straightforward.

FRIDAY 16TH MAY

Today me and Uma went to Oxford. To visit the university. I would never have gone if it wasn't for Uma offering to back me up, I was far too scared. But the world feels different when you show up anywhere with Uma Brunton-Fletcher in her brand new BMW X5 with tinted windows, with your bum all toasty warm and some loud hip hop blaring through the stereo.

I didn't say much for the first thirty miles when Uma was driving me there. I just listened as she gave me one of her amazing lectures about how 'people like us shouldn't feel like we're not meant to be in places like Oxford University'. Uma is really good at this type of thing. She should write her 'lectures' down I reckon and then sell them to people as 'motivational tools'. Our Cava-Sue used to have a book like that which she kept beside her bed when she was at school called *Feel the Fear and Do It Anyway*! Uma's book would be called *Get a Grip, You Knobber* by Uma Brunton-Fletcher. I think it would be a best seller.

'Don't let anyone tell you you're not meant to be somewhere like Oxford, Shiraz!' she was saying. 'Just 'cos people have called me and you chavs, it doesn't mean our brains and our money to pay the fees aren't as good as anyone else's! That university is sitting there and it needs new students. Why not let it be you? Someone has to go there!'

'Mmmm,' I said to her.

'And who deserves a place there more than you?' she said. 'Fenella Flinty-Marmaduke-Handbag or whatever? Some silly cow with a famous father? Some millionth-in-line to the throne member of the Royal family? Oh yeah? Just 'cos someone's great-great-great-great-great-uncle basically stole a load of land off chavvy people in medieval times it doesn't mean they should still be getting all the best things in life now, does it?'

'No Uma,' I said.

'Are you listening to me Shizzle?' she said.

'Yes Uma, of course I am!' I said.

'Do you want me to go in and talk to them with you?' she said.

'NO, Uma!' I said, giggling, 'cos I could just imagine her doing this. Uma is a solid gold hustler. She could probably breeze in and talk them into giving me the letters after my name without even attending at all.

'It makes me cross Shiraz,' she said. ' 'Cos people always think they can put people like us in a box and say, "Oh that's what you're like, that's what you'll do with your life, that's your limits." But it's not. There's no law anywhere that says you and me aren't allowed to be the Prime Minister. Or allowed to start a business and make billions of quid, just 'cos we're chavs, or whatever they want to call us.'

We drove on for a while listening to an old album by the Wu Tang Clan that Uma just got off iTunes. I sat thinking about that for a bit. I hate that word sometimes.

'Are we chavs?' I said to Uma.

I dunno if we are any more.

'Depends who you ask,' Uma said to me. 'I don't think I am. You don't think you are. Cazza and Kez don't think they are either. But if you went into a cocktail bar near mine and Aaliyah's flat in Chelsea and asked some posh kid what Ilford was like then I bet they'd say,' and Uma did her really posh accent, 'Ugh Ilford? How vile!? That whole place is full of chavs! Everyone is a chav! Do you know what chav means? COUNCIL HOUSE AND VIOLENT!'

Uma's posh voice cracks me up. It sounds so totally mad coming out of her mouth. I started remembering then about that time when I was doing AS-levels and I was seeing that lad Joshua Fallow. It was a few years back now. His snobby mother would hardly even talk to me. It did my head in for ages afterwards. I kept remembering how she used to look at me. Like I was scum. She once made me sit on a newspaper in her kitchen as she thought my jeans were probably from Walthamstow market and the dye might rub off and stain her chairs. They were from River Island! She thought that my family must buy everything cheap off market stalls!

Sitting here in the car with Uma, I started to feel quite edgy now. I started worrying that everyone at Oxford University was going to be like Mrs Fallow. Maybe they'd all look at me with big dead eyes when I walked into the room? And they'd all get angry if I put a wet spoon back into the sugar bowl when there are THREE SEPARATE SPOONS for every stage of the tea-making and they shouldn't be mixed up? And they'd ask me questions, just like she did, that she knew I couldn't answer, like, 'Where did your father go to university Shiraz?' Mrs Fallow's favourite trick was to not speak to me at all for the whole time I was standing in the kitchen waiting for Josh to come downstairs, she'd just stare at her copy of *The Observer*, then suddenly spin round and say, 'Shiraz, do me a favour and fetch me some passata from the larder, it's next to the borlotti beans.'

She knew full well there was at least three words in that sentence that were totally alien to a girl from Thundersley Road. It made me feel like rubbish. Oh my dayz, I hated her. And hate is a really strong word. I actually laughed last year when I heard that Josh's father ran off with their cleaner. That's terrible innit? He ran off to live in New York with a twenty-year-old girl from Argentina and now Mrs Fallow is left in her big house all alone with her miserable face and her snobby attitudes and her collection of tea spoons and her stupid hot cupboard thing that never cooked things properly. What was it called? An Aga, that's it.

So I'm thinking all this and then Uma says, 'Shiz, we're nearly here. This is Oxford we're driving into now. The building isn't far from the town centre is it? The sat nav is saying we're about five minutes away.'

'OK,' I said. My stomach was doing big squelchy gurgles. Over and over again.

'Are you all right?' Uma was saying to me.

'Yeah I'm fine,' I said.

'What are you thinking about?' she said.

'Oh God . . . Joshua Fallow's mother,' I said.

'Who?' said Uma, 'Oh that woman who my Zeus went in her kitchen and weed up the front of her oven?'

'Yeah!' I said, 'I forgot about that!' And then we both started howling with laughter.

'My Zeus always keeps it real doesn't he?' she said.

'Tru dat,' I said. Then we pulled up in the little entrance outside the Lord Rothesmere Building and I jumped out and went inside.

The next few hours were really weird. Good but weird. I went to room 5.1.8 and met a man called Dr Tarquin Howard, who I was expecting to be a big scary man who would hate me as soon as he looked at me, but he wasn't at all. He was a small man, about seventy, with white hair and slightly mad eyes and a long grey moustache. He looked like one of the people who guesses the prices on *The Antiques Roadshow*. He made me sit in his study which had about seven million books in it covering every inch of the wall and he made me chat with him about Charlotte

Brontë and Jane Austen and that time years ago when Prince Charles came to visit Mayflower Academy. And he wanted to know what it was like living in Goodmayes and where I want to be in twenty years' time.

So I told him I wanted to be in a place where I could make some of the rules about life because I think that the world is massively unfair.

Well he laughed when I said that and said that Oxford University was a good place for me as they've had many many former students end up in positions of power here. In fact, he said, they've had many people far, far, far less intelligent than me end up running the country. I thought he was joking when he said that so I giggled, and then I realised he was being serious.

Then he asked if I thought it was too early to have a small glass of port so I said, 'Do what you want bruv, it's your study!' Dr Howard smiled and said, 'That's a very salient point, Miss Wood,' then he poured us both a tiny glass and it was like very very sweet thick red wine.

So then we sat for about another half hour chatting and I kept waiting for the real interview to begin, but then he said, 'Well, it's been lovely meeting you and I hope I meet you again if you make the requisite grades. Good luck in the future. I think you would be very content at Oxford.'

'Thank you,' I said and then I shook his hand and I left and wandered back to find Uma in the car park. She was listening to some music and reading *The Financial*

Times and she said to me, 'What just happened then?'

'Do you know something bruv,' I said, 'I'm really not sure, but that old geezer was amazing.'

Then we drove home and I was thinking to myself I would be 'very content' at Oxford. I don't know why. I just felt at that point like I would.

Well, this is where it all gets a bit complicated. Uma drove me all the way back to Goodmayes 'cos she decided to go and drop in and see her mother Rose. Uma doesn't make many 'social calls' to Rose, but it's all a bit more messy now that Kez has had a baby with Uma's brother Clinton, 'cos that means Uma is aunty to Saxon and Uma wants to see him.

Kez happened to be taking Saxon round to see 'Granny Rose' tonight 'cos she thinks it's important Saxon forms a bond with her before Clinton gets out of prison. Uma thought it was best if she drove to Goodmayes and saw everyone at once. When Uma was telling me this I felt like saying that Saxon would be better off forming a 'strong bond' with the old duffer outside Ilford X-change who sells *The Ilford Bugle*, 'cos at least he doesn't sell drugs and have a history of neglecting children, but I didn't want to state the obvious to Uma and to be honest, I felt sorry for Kez 'cos at least she's trying to give her little boy a proper family.

Well anyway, me and Uma were gossiping about all of this as we were driving back into Ilford and then suddenly

I saw something out of the car window that almost totally killed me. It was Wesley. My Wesley Barrington Bains II sitting in the window of Monroe's Wine Lodge with Carly Carrington. SITTING HAVING A DRINK WITH HER.

Carly bloody Carrington.

She was staring right at him, with her head on one side, laughing at whatever he was saying and basically FLIRTING with him. In fact if I think back rightly now I think she had her skirt pulled up so he could see her legs!

Well I wanted to jump out of the car at the traffic lights and run into the pub and pour a pint over both of their heads and give her slap around the face, but even though I was really really mad I knew it was a stupid thing to do. She'd probably call the police. If I got lifted by them that would be really heavy. But I was so angry! I kept trying to tell Uma but I couldn't get the words out.

'That's my Wesley!' I was stuttering. 'In the pub with Carly Carrington!' I was starting to cry now. 'He's flipping cheating on me with that hoochie who was at Carrie's party! The one with the silver skirt that wasn't even a skirt! He's in there now! Uma turn the car around. I'm going in there to have it out with him!'

Uma listened to me carefully and she said, 'Shiz, calm yourself down. What you going on about? Wesley was in where? In Monroe's?' Wes drinks in that pub, Shiz. Maybe he was only sitting with her. Chill out for a minute. Come on, let's drive back to your house and work it out from there.'

'No Uma!' I was crying. 'You don't understand. He never said he was going to the pub tonight! He said he thought he'd be staying in. So why would he be in there unless he was lying to me? He never lies to me. Something is going on!'

'Shiraz, you can't kick off if Wes forgot to say he'd changed his plans and went to the pub. That's not really lying,' Uma said to me. Then she said something that really made me feel bad. 'Look, let's be honest Shiz,' she said. 'All you ever do is lie to Wesley. You lie to him all day long. He doesn't know about your A-levels, he doesn't know about your dream to go to uni, he doesn't know about that bare choong doctor from the hospital who you've been e-mailing who e-mails you back!'

'That's not like that!' I said. 'He's just a friend.'

'I know he is . . . so far,' she said to me. I felt really guilty when she said that. OK, James is absolutely gorgeous, and OK, he emails me about every two weeks to find out how my studies are going along. Just as friends though! There is nothing going on.

'But Shiz,' said Uma. 'Fact is that all of the lies you're telling Wes are quite innocent. You're not doing anything bad or wrong. But you're still lying. You said it to me didn't you? You said it to me and Aaliyah. You said I'm living a lie! And if you've got a whole life going on that you can't tell him, it's a bit rich if you go mental that he's forgot to say he was in the pub.'

She's got a way of putting things Uma has. I couldn't

really argue with her. We pulled up outside my house and I was sobbing and wiping it on the sleeves of my hoodie.

'Shiz, come on girl,' said Uma. 'If you really think something's going on with Wes and that stupid girl, then fair enough, pull him up about it.'

'I'm going to!' I said. I felt like getting the bus back up the road and catching them at it. SNOGGING, I BET.

'And if he is cheating,' Uma said, 'then you have to decide whether to dump him or put up a fight for him. 'Cos that's all she is, some stupid girl. You and him have got a well long history.'

'We've been together for years,' I said. 'Well, on and off. But yeah, we've got major history.'

'I know,' said Uma, 'But . . .'

'But, WHAT!?' I said to her.

'I don't know if you've got a future unless you start telling him the truth about stuff either. About who you are really.'

I wasn't speaking much then. My face ached with crying. Uma made us go indoors to my kitchen and get a cup of tea. Then we rang Carrie. Caz said that I was being stupid 'cos she was in the pub with them both right at that moment and so was about five other people. Carrie reckoned that Wes and some of the lads working with him had been doing a job in the Ilford shop and then there was a power cut, so they'd all finished early and headed to Monroe's.

'So has Shiraz got anything to be worried about with this Carly girl?' Uma said.

Well, Carrie had a good think about that and then she said, 'Well, until you said that I would have said "No way" but now I come to think about it, Carly does act really different whenever Wes appears. She's always mentioning him too. Especially now he's making all that money from his business. She likes her nice things does Carly. And he's a bit of a catch ain't he? Own business, got his own flat and car and van and everything. Oh God, I'll give that girl a slap if I think she's trying to make something happen.'

I felt a bit sick when Carrie said that. I made my decision there and then. I'm going to fight for him. Wesley Barrington Bains II is my fiance and he's going to be my husband. And that's how it's going to be forever.

JUNE

MONDAY 2ND JUNE

I can't believe I ever doubted my Wesley. He's not a cheater. In fact, when I had a go at him the day after I saw him in Monroe's he was totally confused.

He didn't even know Carly was flirting with him. Wes thought Carly was just being friendly. He thought Carly was just really interested in plumbing and how to join pipes and fit extra valves.

'Wesley!' I said to him, as we were lying on his sofa. 'NO GIRLS are interested in hearing about that. Well maybe one or two but not flipping Carly Carrington. The only joining she's interested in doing is joining her face to yours in a massive SNOG.'

Well, Wesley looked proper bewildered when I said that, then he said, 'No, Shiz, I think you're wrong. Carly is always well curious about plumbing, innit. She's always bringing me cups of tea in when I'm working in the shower rooms and asking me stuff! She's just one of them friendly, chatty people innit?'

Tea! Shower rooms? Asking him things? This was getting worse!

'Wesley!' I said to him. 'That's 'cos she fancies you!'

'But she said this morning that she found watching me

bleed a radiator proper fascinating, innit!' Wes said.

'Oh God, Wesley,' I said. 'When I first met you I pretended for the first two years that I loved hearing you do human beatbox.'

Wes looked even more confused then.

'You don't love me doing human beatbox, innit?' he said.

'No, Wes,' I said. 'I'm sorry, I don't. But we're engaged to be married now, so I think we're at a point where we can say this stuff.'

'But, Shiraz,' Wes said. 'You used to say if you shut your eyes, you actually thought there was a real drum machine playing or a helicopter going past, innit,' he said to me.

'I know,' I said. 'Well I fancied you like crazy!'

By now I totally believed that my Wes wasn't at fault in this thing 'cos his face was so flipping confused and innocent that all I wanted to do was cuddle him, not chuck twenty questions at him. We lay there on the sofa for a bit. I kept holding my hand up in the beam of sun that was coming through the window so the diamond in my engagement ring caught the sun and sparkled.

'This is a right headbend, innit,' said Wesley. 'I never know what's going through a woman's head ever.' I didn't argue when he said that, he doesn't. 'And I think you've got it wrong about Carly, innit,' said Wesley. 'She knows I'm engaged! She was asking about it the other day?'

'What was she asking?' I said to him, feeling myself get cross again.

'Well she was saying that it's proper amazing how we stay together and that we must have loads in common deep down, what with us seeming so different, innit.'

'What did she mean by that?' I said. Ooh this girl was crossing a line now! Who is she to question my relationship with my fiancé behind my back? She's got front, I'll give her that!

'Erm, what do you mean, what does she mean innit?' Wes said, looking all flummoxed. 'I don't know what she meant.'

'Is she saying that me and you ain't suited?' I said.

'Er, is she?' he said. 'I never thought of it like that innit! Anyway Shiz, I don't care what she thinks. I love you babe, stop stressing. There ain't no other girls in the world aside from you. You're my world princess innit.'

I decided to leave him alone then. It wasn't really Wesley's fault what Carly was up to. I'd made my point. But I do keep thinking about what she said about me and Wes having loads in common but being totally different. She is seriously disrespecting me by saying it to my fiancé. But the bad thing is I know she's right.

TUESDAY 10TH JUNE

I did my second English A-level paper today. It was fine. No total nightmare questions anyway, but then I must have read about a thousand past years' questions when I was sitting by my mother's bed back in March. I used to sit there when she was looking really at death's door, wheezing 'cos her lungs were totally infested with that virus thing and I'd just try to focus on reading my novel or anything else a bit complicated. It was the only thing that kept my head sorted when I was thinking she might die. Well, that and the sight of Dr Okalleko when he used to wear his tight black trousers. Those times I was pretty much just staring at his hot little bum. (I've decided it's OK for me to think about Dr Okalleko's hot bum as long as I just 'think' and never do anything about it. Which I won't. It's not like I'm showing up at the hospital each day and pretending to be interested in medicine and asking HOW he switches the beep machine on and off then telling him it's fascinating then making him tea. AM I CARLY CARRINGTON, EH?)

Anyway, all the extra reading really paid off. The exam was quite smooth. I think my timed essays went OK too. Proper well argued they were. Not like they'd just been shouted on to the page by a crack-head, which is the kind of thing I was handing in last September. I've come a long way this year. I feel quite clever. Well, a bit clever anyway.

Maybe the exams are going so smoothly 'cos a lot of the pressure has lifted now that I've made my choice about the whole uni thing. I won't need As and Bs if I'm just going to stay here in Goodmayes. I probably won't need exams at all.

In fact, Wes was chattering on today about putting a word in for me down at Tanorife, just to do part-time until we get married and start a family. Wes says if I worked there then I wouldn't have to worry about him chatting to Carly Carrington, 'cos I'd be right there with them every day. I said I'd think about it. I'm not keen on Tanorife to be honest. I went there with Carrie when we got a 50% discount voucher. We went to get a 'honeykissed Hollywood look' for a night out. Well, all I ended up with was a burned right bum cheek and a verruca. It weren't what I was hoping for, put it that way.

When the exam finished today I left Mayflower really quickly 'cos I didn't want to bump into Ms Bracket. I don't think she'd approve of my staying-in-Goodmayes plan at all. I bet she'd say she was 'disappointed' and start going on about my 'dream' and 'fulfilling my potential' and all that kind of stuff she says when she's trying to get kids to do stuff. But the thing is, I'm an adult now not a kid. I make my own decisions. I've chosen to stay and that's that.

THURSDAY 12TH JUNE

I was revising today for my History paper when Isabella from *GMTV* phoned me 'for a catch up' and just to check whether 'me and Lesley the third' were still in love.

Lesley the third. Ha ha ha.

'Of course we're still in love. We've never been more in love,' I said, trying to forget the fact that I spent four hours last night sitting in his van in a driveway in Aldershot Road,

Leyton while he dealt with an emergency sewage pipe overflow. 'Why do you ask that anyway?' I said to her.

'Oh, thank heavens,' she said. 'It's just that one of the other couples has split up so they've had to drop out. Lisa-Jane Howard and Curtis Kelly from Sidcup are no longer in the competition. You're down to the final two!'

'Oh,' I said.

'So it's getting very close now!' she said. 'I hope you've not made any big plans for August? This wedding is almost yours!'

'No,' I said. 'I'm free. We both are.'

'Are you OK?' she said, 'You sound a bit, er, tired or something. Have I just woken you up?'

'No, no,' I said. 'I'm fine. Really. I'm really excited. It's just, like, more of an internal excitement at the moment. I'm trying to keep a lid on it 'cos I don't want to go BANG and get over-excited or nothing.'

'Oh? Oh I see! HA HA HA!' she laughed. 'Well that's good! I was worried for a moment there.'

'What happened to Lisa-Jane and Curtis?' I said.

'Oh, it's quite messy I'm afraid,' she said. 'He dumped her. Curtis came home early yesterday and found Lisa-Jane dying the hair on her head and . . . erm, well, other hair on her body blonde. He thought she was a natural blonde you see. But it seems she was more like a mousy brown.'

'He dumped her for that?' I said, 'What a pig!'

'Well, I think it was the fact she'd been lying to him for

all that time,' said Isabella. 'Trust is so important in a marriage isn't it? It was the fact he thought he knew everything about her but he didn't. He said you can't build a life together based on a foundation of lies.'

'Mmmmm,' I said, doodling a picture of Satan wearing a Lidl shirt on the corner of my History revision notes. 'Alrighty then ... well I'm kind of busy now Isabella so I've got to go.'

'No problem,' said Isabella. 'I just thought I'd tell you. The results are announced at the end of the month.'

'Hang on,' I said. 'Who's left in the competition now, then? Is the girl with one foot still in it?'

'Hold on, I'll look at my notes,' Isabella said. I could hear her shuffling pieces of paper, then shouting to ask someone sitting behind her.

'Then another woman's voice said, 'Yeah Isabella, Pegleg and Dog Biscuit Woman are the two semi-finalists.'

'Pardon?' I said.

'Er, yes,' spluttered Isabella. 'You and Buttercup Bettany, the woman who lost a foot in a gardening accident are the semi-finalists! OK better go now Shiraz BYEEEEE!'

I was going to tell Wes and my mother and Carrie the great news, but as I said, I'm trying to keep my excitement at a minimum right now.

I don't want to peak too early.

197

OK, that was a bit of a weird one. That History exam paper was actually quite, well, all right. I thought they might have slung some nasty stuff in there, but it was all ideas I'd sort of worked on before. I think it helps that I love the Elizabethan period. Flipping LOVE IT. Queen Elizabeth the First was FIERCE. Proper up-town top-ranking sort of bird.

If I could go back in a time machine to another historical period I would definitely choose the sixteenth century in Britain, 'cos London was really exciting and in the grip of all kinds of political and religious change.

Plus we were always going off and 'discovering' new countries. Well, I say 'discovering'. Basically we used to rock up there in boats to places that had foreign people in them already and steal the whole country and kill most of them, then put a British flag up and say, 'Sorry this is ours now, jog on bruv!' And nowadays in Britain we have the cheek to get angry if one little tiny person like Ritu wants to stay in Essex without the right bloody paperwork!

I didn't write any of this in the exam paper today of course, I just stuck to some boring sensible points about how we handled the Spanish Armada.

I asked my Wes the other day which historical period he would go to if he had a time machine and he thought for a bit and said, '*Baywatch.*' I tried to tell him that

Baywatch isn't a historical period, it was just a TV show in the nineties but he couldn't get his head around it and then he said, 'Yeah you would say that Shiz, you just don't want me to go there 'cos all the women wear tiny little red swimming costumes and have well massive boobs, innit.'

He really annoys me sometimes.

MONDAY 23RD JUNE

Oh my dayz. That was my final Film Studies paper. I just walked out of Mayflower Academy for the last time EVER. I just walked out and tried not to look back and get emotional. I just wanted to get away. I don't want to think about it any more. I really loved doing those A-levels. What a mental thing to say eh? But I just did. It felt like I was really pushing my head further than it's ever gone before. It was worth all the sneaking about and the stupid costume changes and the lying. Yeah, even the lying. White lies of course.

I used to really like doing my Film Studies A-level 'cos we had a little room that was really like a big cupboard where we were allowed to watch DVDs for our essays. Proper cosy we made it. We pestered the school to buy us some bean bags in and a little armchair and a heater. I had some amazing afternoons in there watching films by foreign directors like Louis Malle and Pedro Almodovar and Lars Von Trier. Films that bent your head a bit 'cos they were about lives in other countries I'd never normally think about. I'll miss that I reckon.

I walked home back to Thundersley Road and got in the shower and put some make-up on and then my Wes came round to pick me up and take me for a night out. We were going to go bowling but Wes had decided he really wanted to go down Vue cinema 'cos he wanted to see *Bad Pineapple* which is a comedy about these two guys who get so wasted they forget where they live and then they have to try and find their house for the next one hundred and eighty minutes. It got five stars in *Nuts* magazine. Wesley really really loved it and he's going to buy the DVD with all the extras but I didn't think it was that good.

Thank God it's nice and warm in Vue 'cos I just curled up and put my coat over me and had a little sleep.

FRIDAY 28TH JUNE

It was the special VIP opening of the Romford *Tanorife* store tonight. Me and Wes were invited. They had cocktails and a cake and there was some celebrity guests. Kim Bristol who used to go out with Luke Marsh who plays for Queen's Park Rangers was there. She was in that show on ITV2, *WAG Attack!* That show where they give two WAGs five hundred quid each and they both had to buy a skirt or some shoes in under an hour. Carrie used to love it. She used to Sky⁺ it every single week. Oh and one of the Chuckle Brothers was there. Barry Chuckle.

He's the little Chuckle Brother. The less good-looking Chuckle Brother. Oh my dayz, I just said the Chuckle Brothers are good-looking!

Anyway it turns out Barry Chuckle was friends with the man who supplied all the lighting and he just happened to be in Romford that night so he came along. I felt a bit sorry for him really, 'cos Bezzie and Wesley were quite tipsy and they kept shouting, 'To me! To you! To me! To you!' at him so he left after about an hour.

I felt well happy for Collette Brown tonight 'cos she's really done well for herself. She's started building herself a little tanning empire even though she's got kids and she's on her own with them. Her and my sister Cava-Sue get on really well again now, even though they're totally opposite sorts of people personality-wise. They always have their kids to gossip about. Oh and the times back in the day when they used to go down Faces in Gants Hill (although my sister goes quite red when I mention that and says that a lot went on back then that she'd like to forget about altogether!).

Carly Carrington was there tonight and she was on her best behaviour, being really, really nice to me. Too nice. I don't trust her one little bit. She's friends with Wesley and Carrie and they say she's harmless so what can I do? I just try and be 'pleasant', as my mother would say. I find the Tanorife girls a bit hard work sometimes. They're nice and everything but . . . oh, I don't know. At one point Wesley went off to talk to some local business big-wig geezer about some new contract that he wants to pitch for, and he left me with some of the Romford Tanorife girls: Alessina, Mazzia, Izzy, Rai-Rai and Dew. I don't know why Collette only seems to employ people with names that sound like flavours of Mountain Glade air freshener, but whatever. So I stood in the corner with them for about half an hour and they were all gossiping and I was listening and trying to join in but it was really hard. For the first ten minutes they talked about the Bums and Tums class which they all do on Wednesdays but they don't think is that good really 'cos it tones you a bit but it ain't as good as 'spinning' down Spright's Gym, but that's only good when it's Kevron who does it, 'cos he plays some good choons.

Then Dew said that she likes doing some freeweights but not that heavy 'cos she don't want to look too 'unfeminine' and then everyone gossiped about a girl from Bums and Tums who was unfeminine and they all said that she'd never get a bloke 'cos she looks like a bloke herself. In fact she'd have to get a gay bloke but then that wouldn't work out either. And then for the next twenty minutes they worked out who was going to pick each other up in what car next Wednesday for Bums and Tums and in what order the lift would go. But then Rai-Rai said she'd probably not go down Bums and Tums 'cos she was going to go to spinning that week instead 'cos it was Kevron that week and he plays some good choons.

Well then everyone started talking again about Kevron and his 'good choons' and whether his spinning was as effective for toning as Bums and Tums and by this point I wanted to shout, 'THIS IS WHERE THE CONVERSATION BEGAN HALF AN HOUR AGO!' but I didn't 'cos I knew they wouldn't like it. Then they talked about shampoo for twenty minutes, about which ones make your hair bouncy and which ones make your hair straight. I was starting to feel a bit depressed then, but suddenly one of them said, 'What shampoo do you use Shiraz?' and I sort of jumped with fright and said, 'Head and Shoulders!' 'cos that's what I'd used before I came out. It was the first bottle I saw on the shower shelf. I think Lewis has dandruff or something.

'Head and Shoulders!?' said Rai-Rai pulling a face like I'd just said, 'I rub old dog turds into my scalp actually, bruv.'

'Hahahhahah! She's pulling your leg Rai-Rai,' said Dew. 'Oh, Wesley says we're going to have to watch you when you start working here! He says you've got a right old random sense of humour!'

And then everyone laughed at my amazing joke and then they all discussed what locker I could have in the cloakrooms when I begin, which probably sounds like it would only be a conversation that could last three sentences but they managed to make it last at least eighteen minutes.

Then they said I should come down to spinning with

them but only on the night that Kevron is on. Apparently he's got some really good choons.

MONDAY 30TH JUNE

I was walking along throught the Ilford X-change today when my mobile started ringing and I could see right away it was my mother. It freaks me right out if my mother ever rings me on my mobile 'cos I know it must be something important. My mother hardly ever rings a mobile phone, 'cos she still thinks it costs ten pounds per minute and even if she does she says everything she needs to say in about thirty-seven seconds, without breathing.

'Mother, are you all right?' I said. All I could hear was puffing and panting. Oh my God, I thought. She's having a massive relapse! She's on the living-room floor and her lips are blue and she's fallen on to the phone and accidently called me! 'Mother!' I said. 'Speak to me!'

'Shiraz!' she panted, 'Shiraz!'

'What? What's up? Are you OK?' I said.

'Yes I'm OK! I'm blinding! I'm blooming wonderful! Ooh OK, mobile phone – this'll cost the earth! In a nutshell, Glo just heard on the interweb that the woman with the missing foot has been disqualified for cheating from the *GMTV* wedding competition 'cos it turns out she's been messing with the text vote 'cos she knows someone at the phone company and that means she's broke the rules! So her and her bloke have been slung out and that means you and Wes are the only ones left, so I just called up the telly people and they've just said that you're the winner! You've won the wedding. You and Wesley have won! YOU'VE WON THE WEDDING! YOU'VE WON! YOU'VE WON! Oh ain't it amazing! Ain't it?'

'Yeah,' I said, feeling a bit sick all of a sudden. 'It's, well, a real shock.'

I'm getting married on Saturday August 16th.

Oh. My. Dayz.

JULY

FRIDAY 4TH JULY

Me, Kez and Carrie are meeting Phillippe, the 'Win a Wedding' wedding co-ordinator, today to choose my twenty-grand designer couture gown. I feel a bit weird 'cos I've never, ever really dreamed about having a big white wedding dress before. I always thought if I got wed it would be on a beach when I was about thirty and I might just wear a little sundress, but that doesn't seem to be happening now. It's happening in about six weeks and in a church and I'm getting a ginormous dress with a big long train thing on the back and everyone is so psyched up about it that I don't seem to be able to put my foot down.

I said to my mother this morning that I'd maybe just get something a bit classy, like a straight cream frock and maybe a little silver tiara, but my mother looked at me like I'd actually stood on the table and weed on to her Sugar Puffs.

'Shiraz, they're offering to buy you a proper wedding dress!' she said. 'One like Princess Diana wore? Like the one your nan has a photo of her wearing in a frame on top of her telly! Oh, didn't Princess Diana, God rest her soul, look pretty in that? Like a fairy on top of a Christmas tree!'

So I said to my mother, 'But I don't want to look like a fairy! I want to look like me!'

My mother just tutted then and said, 'Shiraz, this is the most important day of your entire life, what do you wanna look like you for? This should be the one day you don't look like YOU! 'Ere, and see what Phillippe can do with your hair, too. See if they can put it in a beehive and stop it being so straggly.'

Well I stopped speaking then, 'cos I didn't want to get into an argument, not that it mattered 'cos my mother was already on the phone to Phillippe with a list of her ideas for make-up, shoes, earrings and flowers.

At some level, I reckon my mother thinks that she's the one getting married.

SATURDAY 5TH JULY

Oh, brilliant. I seem to be getting married in a dress that makes me look like one of the carnival floats on Goodmayes Parade Day. Y'know, when they basically just get a truck and then stick a million pieces of glitter and toilet paper to it? Like that! I'm ringing the shop now to tell them to cancel it. Or at least take a few metres of that sparkly stuff off the back of it. You know who I'm blaming for this? Kezia and Carrie. We got to the shop yesterday and the snooty assistant woman said, 'Oh, so you're the competition winner? Would madam like a flute of Champagne?'

'Yeah, we would,' said Kez. 'Actually, just bring the bottle, bruv.'

So then Kez and Carrie started guzzling Champagne and bursting into tears any time I came out of the fitting room.

'Oh my dayz, Shiz,' Carrie kept sobbing. 'You look like a bride! A proper bride! Like one out of a magazine! Oh, I'm coming over all emotional! All these years we've known each other and now one of us is getting married!'

'I know, it's magic,' said Kez.

'I mean, obviously,' said Carrie, 'I always thought it would be me first. What with me being the one who always got all the boys. But I know my time will be soon! I know my Bezzieboo will get me a ring soon!'

So Kezia started creasing up saying, 'Yeah right Cazza, what's Bezzie gonna buy you a ring with? Man dem gonna swap it for a twelve-inch Pepperami Hot? HA HA HA!'

And then Carrie and Kez started arguing and the snooty woman took their glasses away and hurried me into making a choice on my gown, so I chose the least enormous one with the smallest amount of sparkly jewels on it. But it was still HUGE and it's still going to be HUGE no matter how many feathers and beads I asked Phillippe to ask the snooty woman to take off the headdress.

I showed my mother a picture of it and she cried with happiness for twenty minutes.

WEDNESDAY 16TH JULY

OH MY DAYZ, I really wish my Wesley would take more of a role in planning this wedding, but he doesn't. He just keeps saying, 'Whatever you want, princess.'

But the fact is I don't know what I want. My head is hurting. Like today for example, Phillippe rang up with a list of celebrities that he wants to invite to the wedding, so I says, 'I don't want any celebrities, Phillippe, I don't really know any either,' I said, 'although I did meet Barry Chuckle once but it was very brief.'

Well Phillippe just sighed when I said that and said he was sorry but he'd already tried Barry Chuckle and unfortunately he's busy. Phillippe said what I need to understand is that I've no choice about inviting celebrities as it was in the contract when I entered the competition. Apparently we need them to make the wedding 'more acceptable' to the TV viewers. Then he went down a list of people who had said 'Yes' and it was someone from *The Bill* who I'd not heard of who always plays a smack-head, and this bloke called Colin who is really famous on YouTube for putting the world record amount of Cheesy Wotsits up his nose (apparently the *GMTV* audiences love him) and someone called Jake, who got through to the final eight on *X-Factor* about four years ago. That was it.

'Amazing,' I said.

'I know, it's not everything I hoped for either,' he said.

I told Wesley all of this tonight and he looked really

sad and I thought it was because he was thinking about how out of control this wedding was getting. But then I sussed it out and I said, 'Wes, you're just sad 'cos Barry Chuckle ain't coming, ain't you?'

Wes just looked at me and said, 'Innit.'

SATURDAY 19TH JULY

My mother has gone CRAZYINSANE down at Westmount Shopping Centre and spent over a grand in under two hours. I just rang her and she was in the food court eating a prawn sandwich, almost hyperventilating, going, 'Oooh, it's proper amazing how much you can spend when it ain't your money, eh Shiraz!? Phillippe has gone pale, he has! He says his boss is going to go mad. I've already spent my budget and started skimming off the money for flowers. Anyway got to go! There's a House of Fraser and a Debenhams and a massive Next that I haven't even started on yet!' Then she hung up on me.

This is a woman who has spent the last five months signed off on incapacity benefit, claiming she can't even spread Dairylea on to a piece of toast 'cos it gives her 'chronic fatigue'.

I can't help feeling I've been conned.

TUESDAY 22ND JULY

I called Uma today. I needed to ask her if she still wanted

to be my bridesmaid 'cos I was choosing the frocks and I didn't know whether to get three or not. I've been avoiding having this conversation with her. I know what she must think about what's going on. About me not going to uni and that. I don't even have to talk to her about it, I know what she thinks.

So I called her number and I took a deep breath and I asked her about the dress and I thought she might shout at me, but she didn't, she just said, 'Look, whatever Carrie and Kez like, just get me that in a size ten, but make sure it's long enough 'cos you know I'm tall. I'll text you my measurements.'

'Aw, cheers Uma,' I said. I felt like crying. It was so good to hear her voice.

'No worries babe,' she said, 'I'm really glad you called.'

I am so glad I rang her.

SATURDAY 26TH JULY

Oh my dayz, this is really getting out of hand now. My wedding is NOT my wedding. It is everybody else's wedding.

We are getting married at St Kevin's Church, with a reception in a massive heated marquee around the back of Goodmayes Social Club. (This is what my mother wants.) We are having roast chicken on a bed of dauphinoise potatoes with red cabbage and sticky toffee pudding for afterwards. (This is what my father wants.)

We are being entertained by The Funky-Train Starlight Band afterwards, who are going to play old-skool hits by Jamiroquai and East 17 (this is what Wesley wants), and then we are going to have fireworks outside in the car park for half an hour while someone plays Vivaldi's *Four Seasons* on a portable stereo (this is what Wesley's mother wants).

The only thing that is happening that I want, is that it's starting at 2pm. Well, OK, I originally wanted it at 3pm but the photographer made me change it to 2pm 'cos we'd miss the 'good daylight' and he is nagging me and Wes to take a break between the church service and the chicken dinner so we can go to Goodmayes Park and take some photos of me in my gown feeding the ducks and of Wes pushing me on a swing. The photographer says this is what people usually want.

WHY????? WHY DOES ANYONE WANT THAT?

I told my mother today that I wanted out of this wedding. I said, I was freaked out by it, but she just said I was getting 'cold feet' and that it's a totally normal thing to feel like that before you get married. So I said to my mother, 'But what if it ain't, Mum? What if I'm making a big mistake?'

She just laughed then and told me to stop blubbing ' 'cos the invites have gone out now and they were proper expensive, thick card with gold embossed printing on them,' and she should know 'cos she chose them.

AUGUST

THURSDAY 14TH AUGUST

I ordered a cup of tea at Mr Yolk's this morning, then I found a table in the corner and sat down with my back to everyone. I just needed my own space for five minutes. Just minutes without someone asking me something about the wedding. Or wanting me to make a choice that turns out not to be not my choice at all. I feel quite weird at the moment. Sort of up and down. My mother says this is normal. 'You're just excited about getting married!' she says.

I was adding some sugar to my tea when Mr Yolk, Mario, himself appeared by the table and put his hand on my shoulder.

'It's you Shirelle?' he said. 'Little Shirelle! You come back to see Mario!?'

I laughed when he said that.

It's SHIRAZ Mario!' I said. He's been told a hundred times. 'And yes, I came especially to see you! Things keeping busy?'

'Yes, yes,' he said. 'Things still going OK. People always need tea and eggs.' I looked around the café and there certainly wasn't an empty table.

'You come at the right time anyway, Shiraz,' he said.

'You want job back again?'

'Here?!' I said.

'Yes, all my Polish girls they go home now,' he said. 'I have job. You could start Monday?'

'Oh,' I said. 'I can't really, Mario. I'm getting married on Saturday. I'm off on honeymoon.'

'Married?! Congratulations!' he said. 'That is good news! Oh I'm happy for you! You were a little girl when you work here and now you're a woman. Time passes so quick.'

'I know,' I said. 'I know.'

'Ha, I remember one boyfriend you had back then!' he said. 'Boy with yellow car. Always want egg sandwich every day same thing. He say innit all the time. Innit. Innit. ha ha ha, innit!'

'That's who I'm marrying,' I said.

Mr Yolk stopped laughing right away then. 'Ah he was a very nice boy,' he said seriously. 'I am very happy for you both.'

I felt myself blushing a bit then.

'But when you get back from honeymoon, you give me a shout about job, yes? No one can gets teacups as nice and white as you.'

'I'll think about it,' I said.

I actually meant that. Anything would be better than Lidl or Tanorife.

So then Mr Yolk disappeared off behind the counter and I got the envelope out of my handbag I'd been meaning to open all morning. It was my A-level results. I opened them and stared. Then I sat for ages wondering if what I could see really affected anything now. Then deciding it didn't.

I passed all of them by the way. I got three As.

FRIDAY 15TH AUGUST

Midnight – my bedroom.

Oh God I've just been on my hen night. I am feeling a bit sick really as I had about five glasses of fizzy wine which is at least three past what I can normally drink without chucking up. I'm lying here on my bed and I'm still wearing my flashing devil's horns and the room seems to be sort of moving around the bed. In fact I keep thinking I might be a little bit . . . no . . . hang on . . . I think it's passed now . . . no I do feel sick oh God hang on a minute . . .

Pgh, OK. That's better.

Better out than in I think. I don't know why I drank so much. Nerves I reckon.

It's all really getting to me now. I nearly flipped out tonight during the dinner when all of a sudden this bloke came into Crazy Hombres where we were having our Mexican meal and he starts saying, 'Excuse me, your car is blocking my car, you need to move it!'

So I start saying, 'I don't have a car!' and he kept saying, 'Yes, you do.' And then when I started getting really angry, he suddenly shouted, 'Ha, you've just been punk'd by MR PYTHON!!' and then he ripped off all of his clothes in one big RRRRRRRRRIIIIIPPPPP and started dancing about holding a basket of tortillas over his dangly bits.

Well Kez, who'd arranged him, Carrie, Cava-Sue, my mum, my nan and Aunty Glo were HOWLING with laughter. But I was just sitting there sort of stunned.

' 'Ere Shiraz, cheer up you miserable cow!' Kezia shouted at me. 'He cost me forty quid he did! Oi, Mr Python, I'll play one of your games! Bring your can of squirty cream over here. Ignore her. We reckon she's bi-polar!' Well the squirty cream games were not a pretty sight, to be honest and I am ashamed of my nan for encouraging them.

Uma turned up in the middle of this. She'd had to work till 10pm at Fortune Fountain. She sat down beside me and asked me what A-levels I'd got so I told her. Then she poured us both another glass of fizzy stuff and she said, 'Here's to you Shiraz Bailey Wood. That is absolutely AMAZING! Goodmayes Girls Run Ting don't they?'

Well I laughed and said, 'Yeah bruv, they certainly do.' I had to be taken home soon after that 'cos I started feeling quite sick.

I hope I'm OK for tomorrow.

SATURDAY 16TH AUGUST

11pm.

I'm curled up in bed now trying to think through everything that happened today. It's a bit of a blur. I remember the make-up lady coming at 8am and starting to paint my face. And how my dress was so big that I had to put the head-dress part on when I was standing in the back yard then walk round the side of the house and get in the limo. Our Penny was barking and standing all over the back. My dad looked really smart in his grey suit and my mother looked like one of the Queen's Ladies-in-Waiting. Proper dolled up she was. She looked amazing. I remember Cava-Sue crying as I got into the car and Kez, Carrie and Uma looking all pretty in their matching pale-pink, strapless dresses with dark red bouquets. The makeup artist did an amazing job on Kez's tattoos, you could hardly see them at all.

There was definitely people waiting outside the church, trying to get a look at me in my dress. And a TV crew, yes definitely one of those. It took me ages to get all of the dress out of the car as it kept getting trapped in the door. In fact Phillippe had to puff it all out for me and straighten my head dress 'cos my hands were shaking. Then my dad linked my arm into his and we walked up to the church then through the doorway of St Kevin's. I could hear all the guests chattering away inside. But then someone must have warned them we were here and it all went SILENT.

Then the organ began to play *Here Comes the Bride* and the big wooden doors flung open and I could see the whole church and EVERYONE LOOKED AROUND AT ONCE. Then me and my dad started to move up the aisle slowly.

Well, faces were a blur now. I'm sure I saw my friends Sean and Danny. I definitely saw Chantalle Strong, Glo, Pat, Nan and Clement, Murphy and Ritu – who were all in the front rows. Murphy was in a navy suit with white trainers and Ritu in a floaty dress with flowers in her hair. And right at the front of the church was my Wesley, stood there in a top hat and tails with his best man Bezzie stood beside him. Wes was looking as nervous as I was Then the vicar stood up and began saying all of this stuff about how great it was that we were all there today to celebrate 'the union of one man and one woman in the eyes of God'. Then he talked about being married and how it is FOREVER and how important that is and how it should never be undertaken 'lightly' or 'ill-advisedly' but instead should always be 'seriously' and 'duly considered in the manner in which it is ordained'.

Well I must say I was feeling well sick by now. Really green. All I could hear was people occasionally coughing behind me and for some reason my mind was floating and I was thinking weird stuff about *Tess of the D'Urbervilles* and about Dr James from the hospital, or whether I'd unplugged my GHDs before I came out of the house.

Then suddenly the vicar said, 'These two persons have come together today to be made one. But if anyone here knows any just cause why they may not be married, then let them speak now or forever hold their peace.'

Well there was total silence when he said that, except for a few people giggling, 'cos that part of the wedding is always funny 'cos no one ever has anything to say and it sounds so dramatic. But then the vicar went to speak again and suddenly someone said:

'I do. I've got something.'

It was Uma! She was stood there behind me, clutching her bouquet, looking really anxious. Like she knew she was in the wrong but couldn't help herself.

'I beg your pardon?' said the vicar.

'I said, I've got a reason.'

'No she HASN'T,' shouted my mother. 'Shut up Uma! I thought your trouble-making days were behind you!'

Well the vicar looked at Uma, then at me, and Wesley and said, 'Well I'm afraid I have to hear this. Please go on.'

Uma looked really nervous, but she took a deep breath and said, 'THE BRIDE IS LIVING A LIE!'

'You what?' said my mother. 'Ignore her, Vicar, she's on crack or something.'

'No I'm not,' Uma said. 'The bride is living a lie! I don't think she wants to get married. She's been doing A-levels secretly! And she's passed them all.'

'What's she going on about?' Wes said. 'Has Uma gone nuts, innit?'

Well the congregation were all beginning to mutter now.

'AND SHE HAS AN OFFER FROM OXFORD UNIVERSITY!' said Uma.

'Right that's it, get her out,' said my mother. 'Once a Brunton-Fletcher, ALWAYS a Brunton-Fletcher!'

Well by this point Phillippe and one of his helpers were stomping up the aisle to remove her and I couldn't let that happen so I shouted, 'IT'S TRUUUUUUUUUE!'

'Which bit?!' shouted Cava-Sue.

'Erm, all of it,' I said.

'But you work at Lidl!' said my dad.

'Only sort of,' I said.

'I thought I could never find you in there, innit!' said Wesley, who looked in deep shock. I really did feel terrible now.

'OK,' said Uma, 'So all I'm saying is . . . I don't think Shiraz should get married.'

Well there was deathly silence then. Wesley's face was starting to look really cross.

'Actually, neither do I,' said Cava-Sue. 'In fact I've thought that all along. I was trying to keep my nose out.'

'OK, now we're being truthful. I don't think she should marry Wes either,' said Kez. 'She's had a face like a slapped arse all week. And dat ain't right izzit?'

My mother looked about to explode now.

'Well thank you very much for all of your opinions everybody,' she said. 'But this is a very important day for me! This is the first of my children to get married!'

'NO IT ISN'T,' shouted Murphy.

'What?' cried my mother, 'What are you going on about?'

'We got married. Me and Ritu. About three months ago,' said Murphy. 'Ritu is my wife. She is legally a British person now. Or something like that anyhow.'

Ritu looked really happy when he said that then she shouted, 'AND I AM PREGNANT! WITH A BABY! It in my belly, right now!'

'Ritu!' said Murphy. 'We said we'd wait till after Shiz's day!'

'Oh sorry,' said Ritu. 'I thought this was tradition, I thought we all shout the truth!'

Well this is about as much as I can remember, 'cos after that it all goes a bit blurry again. Everyone was shouting. And at some point Uma got my hand and we wandered through all of the arguing and walked out of the church doors and I took off my head dress and gave it to a child that was waiting with her mummy to take a photo of me. Then I took the whole dress off and threw it into the boot of Uma's BMW X5 and put one of Uma's hoodies over my white petticoat and we drove out of Goodmayes and towards London to Chelsea. I didn't cry or anything, we just sat there listening to the Wu Tang

Clan and I thought about how happy I was to be going to Oxford University and how I'm going to enjoy every single second I have when I'm there. I really am. I want to let my head expand and be the master of my own destiny and be in a position where people listen to what I think about things. When we got to the flat Aaliyah ran me a bath and made me some hot chocolate and now I'm lying in the spare room in borrowed pyjamas. I've just had a text on my phone from Wesley Barrington Bains II and it was very short but it meant a lot to me, it said:

'I DONT HATE YOU, INNIT. I UNDERSTAND.'

OCTOBER

FRIDAY 3RD OCTOBER

Today is my twenty-first birthday, but I'm not having a party, I'm moving house. I've been up since 7.30am packing my stuff. The last thing I packed was my duvet.

Penny was gutted, she was asleep under it.

Before I packed it, I crept under the covers for a while and me and Penny had a cuddle. She still takes up all the bed. She's not fat, of course, she's just big-boned.

The hairs on her nose are going silver now 'cos she's getting well old too. We lay there in a lump for a while and I said to her, 'Silly fat Pen, I will miss you,' and she licked my ears and at that moment I had a couple of little tears, but I tried to stop them 'cos I didn't want my mother to see me upset, 'cos it would make her upset too.

I took the last bags downstairs and stacked them up in the hallway and rang Dial-A-Van and told them I was ready to go. Murphy was in the living-room eating a Monster Munch sandwich and Ritu was lying on the sofa with her bump poking out of her trousers reading a baby magazine. My dad had just got in from work and he was in his chair reading the Ilford Bugle and my mother was in the kitchen fussing away trying to convince me to carry a small tupperware carton of butter all the way to Oxford 'cos she's worried they won't have butter when I get there. Oh and loo paper too. I wandered through into the kitchen and picked Fin up out of his chair and gave him a big cuddle.

'Maisy Shiz?' he said to me.

'Nah, not Maisy,' I said. 'I've got somewhere to go Fin.'

Just then I heard a van beep outside and my dad get up and start carrying my things to the boot.

Cava-Sue appeared then and looked at me and started to have a little cry. I grabbed her and pulled her to me for a cuddle.

'You're doing the right thing,' she said. 'Don't mind me Shiz, I'm just really really proud.'

'Cheers sis,' I said. She'd made my cheeks all wet with her tears.

' 'Ere Shiraz,' said my mum, as the last of my bags disappeared and I got into the front seat of the van. 'I've been looking at this Oxford place on the map at work. It ain't as far away as I figured. In fact me and Glo could do a day-trip couldn't we?'

'Yes!' I said. 'I hope you do, Mum. I'll miss you.'

'Well we perhaps will,' she said. Then she leaned in through the window of the car. 'Go easy girl. I love you.'

'Love you too, Mum,' I said, holding her hand like a little girl for a bit.

And then the van drove away. As I reached the corner of Thundersley Road I looked behind me and they were all there, in a row, still stood there waving.

* * *

I'm writing this in my new room at Oxford.

It's tiny but it feels quite cosy now I've got all my stuff in. I'm not sure what the heck me, Shiraz Bailey Wood, is doing here at this posh university, but the main thing is I know I'm following my heart and being the master of my own destiny and all that kind of stuff.

Oh and I'm keeping it real.

I'm always keeping it real.

OMG! You've gotta go and check out....

www.shirazbaileywood.co.uk

- ⭐ Read all about what's going on in Shiraz's world in her SLAMMIN' **weekly blog**

- ⭐ Join up to the TOTALLY MENTAL **forum** to meet and chat with other Shiraz fans

- ⭐ Free desktop and mobile phone wallpapers to download

- ⭐ Exclusive BLINGIN' **members' area** for VIPs like yourself

- ⭐ **Have your say** and vote on what's hot and what's not, word of the week and much more... OH MY DAYZ!

Log on today at www.shirazbaileywood.co.uk
You'll be lovin' it – guaranteed!